ROSE'S ONE NIGHT TO FOREVER

HEART FALLS VIGNETTE AND NOVELLA COLLECTION #3

VIVIAN AREND

Rose's One Night to Forever
Copyright © 2022 by Arend Publishing Inc.
ISBN: 9781990674181
Edited by Angie Ramey
Cover Design © Damonza
Proofed by Manuela Velasco & Linda Levy

1

April, Red Boot ranch

Chance Gabrielle was tired of living out of suitcases.

He followed the GPS of his rental car, turning down the rustic driveway. A scene from a country and Western movie lay before him as he stopped in the wide car park outside a small cabin. One of a dozen scattered around the area.

Stepping outdoors, he was assaulted by fresh air and the scent of the spring afternoon. The distant mountains still held snow, but the nearby fields were mostly clear. Brown grasses and open fields flowed toward rolling hills dotted with pine trees of varying heights.

The landscape held grace. A kind of beauty that reminded him of his homeland in Ireland and yet something fresher. Younger. A land that Chance could already sense would suit the man he called *brother* to a T.

It didn't matter how few years they'd had together before Chance had grown up and moved away, that truth had always been clear. His little brother, Cody, was a man of the earth and eager to work with his hands.

Chance's career might be less physically challenging, but it too was full of life and appreciation of beauty. Hopefully, Heart Falls would inspire him and suit him as well as it did his brother.

He turned from the majestic scenery and made his way up the cabin steps.

Before he could knock, the door swung open and a tall man dressed in jeans, boots, and a cowboy hat jerked to a stop in the doorframe.

His stepbrother's expression flashed quickly through surprise and confusion to settle on utter delight. "Chance. Holy *shit*—you're really here."

"I really am," Chance agreed, a smile coming easily. "Gawd, look at you."

Cody caught him in a tight embrace, slapping Chance on the back with enthusiasm. "I had no idea you were coming. Did I miss an email or something?"

"No, I didn't warn you because I wasn't certain I'd be able to pull it off." Chance stepped back and clasped Cody by the shoulders. His brother's eyes were bright, the white skin of his face and hands tanned in spite of just having come through winter. Contentment sat easily on his shoulders. He looked good. "I don't have long, but I wanted to see with my own eyes that you were still kicking."

"I would have told you if it were otherwise," Cody promised with a hint of twisted humour. "Come back as a ghost, or somehow made myself appear in one of your fantasy paintings."

Chance had so much to share, but his brother's quick

glance at his watch warned a drawn-out conversation was not in the books. "I've surprised you, and I'm keeping you from your duties. Can you take a break later for us to chat?"

"How long can you stay?" Cody asked.

"I return to Ireland tomorrow with a weeklong stop in Germany first. My flight's at four p.m."

A snort escaped his brother. "This isn't a visit; it's a flyby."

"Pretty much," Chance agreed. "But I needed to try my luck."

Cody took a deep breath then motioned to the deck chairs outside the cabin. "Let me contact my boss to tell her I'll be late. She won't mind, but I have a site evaluation in an hour with an inspector, and they've been a pain in the ass to schedule. I have to make that one."

"We'll have time," Chance promised.

"In the morning, if nothing else."

Chance waited as Cody made a call, using the opportunity to admire not only the surroundings but how well his younger brother fit into the space. He looked completely at home.

A sharp jab of jealousy struck before being instantly vanquished. Chance wanted nothing but the best for his family. The choice to wander the world and live apart from them had been his own.

The decision to change his mind was also his to make.

Cody settled into the other chair. "Talk fast," he teased before sobering. "It's good to see you. Seriously."

"I would have given you more warning," Chance said, "but I had three different meetings myself. The final gallery thankfully decided I was one step shy of God himself and didn't ask for a single change to my proposal. Which meant, instead of being done tomorrow with barely enough time to head to the airport, I had an extra evening."

"I'm glad you came. Just pissed off that this is one of the few days I'm absolutely booked solid." Cody shook his head. "So tell me—the gallery showing in Calgary. Can you come for a longer stay when that happens? I assume you're still curating shows for your fancy art goddesses and what have you."

"I am, but I have other plans as well." Chance leaned forward, elbows on his knees. "I'm moving."

"Interesting. London? Berlin?" Cody tilted his head. "New York?"

"Heart Falls."

Cody coughed and frowned. "You're shitting me."

Dear Lord. "Your expressions never fail to make me laugh. No, brother, I'm not *taking the piss*, as we would say in Ireland." Chance paused to let out a peal of laughter. "God, your face."

"You're full of surprises today. Moving to Heart Falls." Cody glanced around then back at Chance. "Did you somehow pull me into one of your fantasy pictures? Are we living on the edge of reality, surrounded by the myths and legends of ancient Ireland?"

"I tell you I want to move back to Canada and closer to you, and you think I'm winding you up?" Chance shook his head. "You have no idea how much I look forward to the change."

Cody dipped his head. "Okay. I didn't mean for that to come off as not wanting you around. I'm shocked, though. It's not what I expected, but having you here would be great."

"I'll share more as I figure it out myself. In the meantime, tell me what you've been up to. And show me your couch so I have a place to sleep tonight."

His brother rose to his feet, glancing at his watch. "I can do one step better than the couch. You can have your own cabin for the night. I know they're not fully booked right now."

Chance was led to a cabin a few doors down, and Cody pointed out salient parts of the ranch as they walked. Catching up felt good.

They emailed and messaged occasionally, but living on different continents had made the past few years more hit-and-miss for communication. Chance had missed the daily exchanges they'd enjoyed when young.

"I'll try to get free for dinner," Cody offered, "but, like I said, today is hell. I'm working the afternoon and evening, and I'm on call tonight."

"Oh, you're grand," Chance said. "I'll need a suggestion for dinner, though."

Fifteen minutes later, after a few more quick exchanges and explanations, Cody was gone.

Amusement and contentment settled in Chance's gut. This was going to work out fine. He tucked his hands in his pockets and took himself for a stroll. Wandering the place his brother called home.

His memories drifted to the past. They'd had a few rough moments between them right after Chance's father had fallen in love with Cody's mum—online dating, of all things—and brought the two boys together into one family. Mostly because back then, the age difference meant Cody had followed Chance around like an eager puppy.

Chance had been more interested in teenage exploration of his new Canadian home in Toronto, and having an eleven-year-old kid begging to accompany him on dates was not on his sixteen-year-old agenda.

Still, they'd both grown up, and they'd grown into a solid family. The years since had meant changes, good ones for the most part, but now it was time for the next step.

His stomach growled. Chance dressed as casually as possible from the options he had with him. He left off his suit coat and tie, pulled on a light jacket, then headed to town.

THIS WAS ALL her sister's fault.

Rose Fields lifted the longneck beer and sipped while she took another peek around the dance floor, examining her options.

Okay, maybe standing in her hometown local bar while ogling men wasn't *specifically* Tansy's fault, but after twenty years of being sisters through adoption, blaming each other for imagined sins was more than habit. It was...

Well, family, Rose supposed.

A handsome cowboy approached, smiling with deep approval as he checked her over. "Hey, darling. Want to go for a spin?"

Tommy was a great dancer, and usually she'd have been thrilled to say yes. But he worked at Silver Stone ranch, which meant he was all wrong for tonight's agenda. Too familiar, too local.

Too not-good for a one-night stand.

Rose shook her head and lifted her drink. "Just started my beer. I'll give you a shout later."

He winked. "Sure thing, beautiful."

The pulsing beat of the music echoed around her. It filled her ears and set her toes tapping. Even as she examined the crowd for someone who was just right, her thoughts drifted back to the reason she was in Rough Cut by herself in the first place.

Girls' Night Out Gone Wrong.

Okay, maybe labeling it that was pushing it, but when the larger assembly of girlfriends had dropped to just Rose, her sister Tansy, and two others, out had come those damn confessions. Three weeks later, and Rose was kicking herself for not being able to shake the conversation. The one where the other women in the room had all confessed to being wild and spontaneous. Looking for satisfaction, and finding it in one sensual night.

Not something you have to do, but if you want to do it and the chance arises, why not?

The comment from her friend Petra echoed loudly.

Rose had enjoyed a good, stable upbringing. Her adoptive parents were rock-solid, and her three sisters were golden. Add in the store and café she owned with Tansy, and she had nearly everything she'd ever dreamed of.

Why did she still feel as if the smallest wrong move could make it all vanish in an instant? She needed to stop living so carefully. Wanted to actively seek out adventures and see what might happen.

There lay the reason why she now stood in Rough Cut trying to open the door to opportunities. She wouldn't mind finding a handsome stranger to take for a ride.

So to speak.

One thing was for certain. If she planned to pick up a stranger in their small hometown, it was not going to be under the watchful eye of her sister. Or friends. Or...*anyone.* Which was why she'd come to Rough Cut tonight when Tansy was busy and all her other friends were occupied.

Yet she needed to do this safely, which meant telling someone.

Petra. Petra was perfect. The youngest sister of one of the local ranchers, she didn't actually live in Heart Falls, just visited often. Often enough that she'd become a regular at their girls' nights, including the most recent one that still haunted Rose.

After a wonderful visit where she'd spent time with family and Rose and the others, Petra had returned home to Manitoba two weeks ago. Far enough away that Rose didn't need to worry about the woman showing up to run interference, but connected enough that if Rose put out an SOS, help would be on the way pretty damn quick.

Decided, she messaged her friend.

Rose: *FYI, you're my emergency contact tonight. I'll message you around midnight. If needed, again in the a.m. to let you know I'm safe.*

Less than a minute later, a response slipped in.

Petra: *Okay. Want to tell me what you're doing?*
Rose: *I'm having a one-night stand.*
Petra: *Oh, really? Someone catch your eye to make this an urgent and top priority?*

Rose wasn't about to explain her entire agenda in text. She lifted her attention from her phone to consider the best answer, then the crowd parted and the overhead lights flared like a spotlight to land on a tall, gorgeous man, and everything vanished except him.

Broad shoulders, but lean. Less bulky than most of the cowboys she knew, he still looked sturdy enough to have muscle and strength in all the right places. Taller than her, but not looming. No cowboy hat, but dark, neatly trimmed hair that Rose suddenly wanted to run her fingers through to mess up the tiniest bit. He stood with his shoulders back and chin up, and as he rotated toward her, Rose found herself holding her breath.

His gaze drifted over the crowd then landed on her, and she swore a bolt of lightning sizzled up from the floor.

Green eyes. Intense, but with crinkles at the corners that deepened as his lips curled into a smile. The pale skin on his face was darkened by a five-o'clock shadow. Admiration rose as his gaze dipped quickly over her. No leering, just an honest, masculine appreciation, and Rose checked off another box on her *must have these qualities before I take the leap* list.

He stepped toward her, weaving through the crowd.

Rose quickly finished her message to Petra, happy to be succinct and truthful.

Rose: *Yes.*

2

R ose had barely tucked her phone away when polished black loafers came into view.

"Hello." The faintest hint of an accent coloured the word. "Would you like to dance?"

"Love to." Rose accepted the hand he held toward her.

The fast pace of the two-step he whirled her into didn't let her ask any questions. She focused on enjoying the flex of his shoulder muscles under her fingers as he guided her smoothly across the floor, the music booming around them. She held on and enjoyed the sensation of being led by an expert dancer.

When the third song dropped to a ballad pace, he adjusted his firm grip to a more cradling embrace. His fingers widened on her lower back, and the gentle caress was enough to set the lightning zaps flaring again.

His gaze danced over her face, amusement in his eyes. "You've left me breathless. What's your name?"

"Rose."

His grin widened. "It suits you. I'm Chance. Pleased to meet you."

The fact he didn't start reciting *Romeo and Juliet* after hearing her name was another plus on the list.

No one should reference lines from *that* story when trying to pick up a woman.

"You've got an amazing accent." Rose stroked her fingers over his shoulders and watched his pupils dilate as they swayed together. "Are you travelling?"

"From Ireland. Travelling for work. Art studios, galleries. That sort of thing. You?"

She noted in passing that a man who worked in art galleries was not a candidate to move to Heart Falls. Which meant his response to her answer was the final test.

"I own a flower shop."

Heat flared in his gaze. He dipped his chin then twirled her. When she came back into his arms, he caught her even closer. "Impressive. That's an art form in itself."

Every muscular inch of his body was pressed to hers. He hadn't made a smart-ass comment about Rose selling roses. He knew how to dance. He knew how to *move*.

He smelled amazing. Check off another box on her list.

Rose tossed her hair over her shoulder and focused directly on his eyes. "Want to kiss me?"

Another flash of heat. "More than you can imagine." He glanced around the room. "Here? Now? Go on, but I wouldn't mind some privacy either."

Torn between throwing caution to the wind and enjoying the moment, Rose decided having a bevy of past dance partners come to her rescue might put a damper on her evening plans. "Come with me."

She grabbed him by the hand and went for broke. Her impulsive one-night stand officially started now.

THE INCREDIBLE WOMAN currently leading Chance Gabrielle into temptation had not been on his agenda, but moments like this were what made life exciting and fresh.

From the moment he'd spotted her across the room, a sense of absolute rightness had flooded his system. His stepbrother might have teased Chance about living in a fantasy world, consumed by the art he surrounded himself with, yet this seemed a perfect example of fantasy becoming truth. As if this evening, and more, simply had to be.

Destiny? Fate? Some benevolent being offering him exactly what he'd always longed for?

It wasn't only that she was a beauty and attracted him on a physical level—although she totally was. Light-brown skin that glowed in the golden light of the pub. Dark hair that hung straight down her back and swayed as she turned her head to examine the room. A tall, lithe body that curved and flowed and begged for a man to explore it thoroughly as he brought her to ecstasy.

Her eyes, though. They were what made his feet move of their own accord in her direction. Deep brown in colour and snapping with intelligence. So damn mesmerizing, Chance had decided right then and there that he wasn't leaving without finding out more.

He'd thought *more* might involve a few dances and asking for her contact information so he could ring her when he returned to Heart Falls in the summer. Being close to Cody was one goal. Having someone like Rose to spend time with in the future?

The thought was beyond motivating.

She appeared to have more on her mind than a few dances and an exchange of numbers, though. Hell if he would argue with a woman who knew her own mind.

He held her hand and followed as she paced from the dance floor toward a dark corner of the room.

Still not his favourite place to take things up a notch physically, but he'd have a better chance of convincing her to come back to his temporary digs at the Red Boot ranch after a few kisses.

Confident? Hell yes. He was going to bring his A game.

When she paused, he reached for her then stalled as she opened a nearly invisible door and slipped through, gesturing for him to follow.

Even as she closed the door, Chance took in their surroundings. They briefly stood on a small landing under a pale-yellow light before she led him up a narrow staircase along the outside wall of the building.

Suddenly it all made sense.

"These buildings are all connected, aren't they?" He'd noticed the old-fashioned setup while eating dinner at the excellent Korean restaurant across the street. "All the fake-fronted shops along the wooden boardwalk in the Heart Falls town centre are connected. And there's housing above them—"

Rose shoved open a door and tugged him with her. An instant later, she fisted the front of his shirt in her hands and brought their bodies together. "Architectural discoveries later."

Good point. Chance smiled down, eyeing her lips. He cupped her face with his hands and leaned closer. "Kisses now, yes?"

"Yes." The word came out breathless. She opened her palms and smoothed his shirt, heat passing between them. "Very much, yes."

He caught the final word against his mouth.

The urge to sweep in and possess was strong, but the lovely fantasy maiden the gods had gifted him deserved more. He jerked himself under control and slowed to seduce her.

Soft, gentle. The touch between them a barely there contact that echoed the way her skin felt against his hands. Mysterious and taunting. A silken caress that made his fingertips tingle and excitement slide down his spine.

Her mouth was molten velvet, giving and sweet as he angled her head to the side and teased his tongue past her lips. The rush of pleasure that swamped him at tasting her felt right. Felt as if he'd been waiting forever for this moment to arrive. For something—no, *someone*—he'd known was out there but had only dreamed he'd someday meet.

Slipping his left hand back, he stroked his thumb over the smooth heat of her cheek. A shiver took her as he eased his fingers through the silky strands of her hair to cradle the back of her head.

Keeping her close, his right hand drifted to her lower back, and he pressed their torsos flush. All the while he kissed her. Tasted her. Learned what it took to make her moan.

The point of contact between their lips was addictive. The sensation of her hands drifting over his torso upped the ante and made him tremble in return.

When she put her fingernails on his back and slowly clawed downward, branding him through his shirt, he broke the contact between their lips with a gasp. "Christ. I want more."

"Good. Let's go for more."

The smile on her lips was slightly smug for some reason, but hell if he cared why.

Chance glanced around the room she'd pulled them into. Not a home but a storage facility of some kind. Shelves lined two walls, and tables rested here and there, all visible in the pale glow of the streetlight directly outside the window. The faintest hint of dust lay on the floor, which made him question the cleanliness of the overstuffed easy chairs in the corner.

Not the place he'd choose to make this woman sing with pleasure.

He stroked his fingers through her hair and met her gaze,

speaking in a low rumble that exposed just how turned on he was. "Come to my room. I have a cabin for the night at the Red Boot ranch."

He could have sworn interest flashed in her eyes when he first spoke, but mention of the ranch wiped it clean.

Rose lifted her hand, caressing her fingers over his lips. "Here is good. We can get creative."

Creative he could do. Although at some point, once he was back in Heart Falls for good, Rose and a good long session in his bed were absolutely in the plan. Multiple times. Plus whatever else might be in the works for them in the future.

He leaned his shoulders on the wall behind him. "Creative it is."

With Rose between his legs, he adjusted position until he was free to drop his fingers to the buttons of her blouse.

Her cheeks flushed, and as he slipped the second button free, her tongue flicked over her lower lip and her gaze fixed on his mouth. "I like how you kiss," she confessed.

"I plan to kiss you a lot of other places before we're done."

He'd gotten the final button open and now took a deep, appreciative breath. So much glowing skin revealed as he peeled back the soft-blue blouse. The bra that lovingly cupped her pert breasts was also pale blue lace, and hints of her delectable skin peeked through with the loveliness of a mist-painted forest scene.

"Beautiful." He glanced to the side, thankful to spot a straight-back chair within arm's reach. He eased the blouse from her shoulders, leaning in to kiss her neck and lower as he draped the fabric over the chair without looking.

Rose moaned as he licked a slow line along the edge of the lace. "Don't stop, but can I mention I appreciate you not dropping my clothes on the floor?"

"I live to serve." He popped the clasp of her bra, groaning when the fabric fell away and her dark nipples came into view. "You're an angel and temptress in one gorgeous package."

Her bra joined the shirt on the chair, and he draped her over his arm, licking a slow, enviable path to the peak waiting taut and ready for his mouth.

Rose shuddered and clutched his shoulders as she arched and lifted her breasts higher, begging for his mouth. "It's good. *So* good."

He agreed, planning to draw this out and enjoy himself. Enjoy her. Only a moment later, she tugged at his shirt, pulling herself upright and away from his questing lips.

"Clothes off. Now," she demanded.

Naked took longer than she probably expected. Oh, he tugged his shirt over his head in a split second, stripping it away while he marched quickly to make sure the door they'd come through was locked. He was back nearly instantly, shoving off his pants before jamming his feet back into his shoes. His boxers lifted with the swell of his cock as he switched their positions.

Rose's back was to the wall, hands pressed to the vertical surface near her hips. Chance knelt in front of her, staring in appreciation as he eased off her pants and slipped them past her feet.

She laughed softly when he held out her half boots and guided her feet back into them. "We're having sex with our shoes on?"

"Seems prudent," he admitted, pausing to take a deep breath before dealing with the final bit of unwrapping.

The pale undies glided down her long legs like a whisper of prophecy.

Something wonderful was about to happen.

3

Chance tilted his head back and smiled at the lush woman now naked above him. "You said something about kisses."

Rose's eyes widened, and then he couldn't see her face because it was all about her skin, satiny and smooth under his lips. A kiss to her belly, to the notch where her torso and leg met.

To the sweet, dark curls gracing her sex.

She stroked her fingers through his hair. "*Chance.*"

"Hold that thought," he ordered. He tapped the inside of her thigh, and she willingly widened her stance. The soft lips of her labia were just visible, and he pressed closer, exploring with his mouth.

Her taste exploded onto his tongue as she tilted her hips and opened farther, all but begging for more. Begging for what he was desperate to give.

Easing between her folds, he edged upward until he could taunt the small bud of her clit. Stroking it with the tip of his tongue before working downward. Again and again. Driving both of them in the right direction.

Chance licked two fingers then gently slipped them into her sex. Rose's groan of pleasure echoed in the empty room, egging him on, pushing his control to the limit as he once again closed his lips around her clit and sucked. He gently stroked the front of her passage until he found the sweet spot that made her gasp.

Then he did it again, one hand anchoring her against the wall as her hips bucked against his face.

"Chance. I'm so close."

"Let go."

The fingers tangled in his hair tightened, and Rose tugged sharply as her throaty cry rang out. Her sex tightened around his fingers, her moan and full-body quiver filling him with pride.

Pride and a hellish need.

He was on his feet, losing the boxers quickly before turning her in his arms. Her back to his front, naked skin sliding together, his cock a rock-solid line against her buttocks.

Chance pressed his hand over her belly to firmly retake possession of her mound. He teased his fingertips over the slick wetness of her clit and pussy, extending the pleasure of her orgasm as he savoured the heat between them.

It was another moment of perfection. The faint light in the curtainless room combined with the darkness outside the windows, creating a mirror effect. He'd turned them toward the outside wall when he'd captured her against him, and now a glorious image shone back. Him holding her upright with her long hair flowing over her shoulder, her hands clutching at his wrist as he played his fingers through her wet folds.

Outside the building was darkness and the faintest hint of stars. A show only the two of them could see.

"I could sell this picture for a million dollars, but it's worth more than that. It's priceless, unique, and *mine*." The possessive growl in his tone shocked him. Chance took an uneasy breath, fighting to regain control.

Rose lifted a hand and draped it around his neck. After turning her face toward him, she pressed her lips to his cheek. Hungrily, he took her lips again. Still playing with her, edging her up toward another masterpiece that, this time, he would join and they'd create together.

She nipped at his lower lip. "Condom."

"Yours or mine?"

A beautiful smile bloomed on her face. "Mine."

She twisted far enough to pull what they needed from her pants. He stole the package from her, all concentration as he covered himself. His hands shook slightly as she turned and pressed kisses over his chest, his shoulders, stealing his brain as she entwined around him. Skin touched, brushed. Teased.

The instant he was ready, he spun her to face away from him again then lifted her to kneel on the low table with her knees wide, the heated core of her lined up perfectly.

He slipped into her from behind.

Sweet paradise surrounded him. Physical pleasure was there as skin caressed skin, she enveloped him, and he pushed deep on each stroke.

But that window—

The image clearly reflected the pleasure on her face, her gaze locked on where their bodies connected. He circled his fingertips over her clit and her head fell back, landing on his shoulder.

"Yes. That's so good."

He groaned, words failing as release beckoned. A throaty moan escaped her throat. A pulse of her hips against his hand, then the grip around him tightened as she came again.

She tore a response from him, his orgasm rushing in. The world went blurry, and his legs shook with the bliss of it.

Chests heaving as they gasped for air, Chance cradled her

tight and somehow kept his footing. That had been fantastic, and he couldn't wait to do it again.

He nuzzled the side of her face with his nose. "How are you keeping?"

She laughed. Soft and lusty and with one hundred percent approval. "Very well."

"I need to take care of the condom."

She waved a hand toward the right wall. "Bathroom's there."

"You want it first?"

This time her amusement was louder. "I think your need is greater than mine right now."

Truth. He kissed her cheek then stepped back far enough to slip from her body. They both made noises of disapproval.

Yes, they were absolutely doing this again as soon as possible.

Chance helped her off the table and made sure she had her balance before letting go. "I'll be right back. Don't go away."

He took one step before something warm smacked him briefly on the butt. He flicked a glance over his shoulder to discover her grinning widely as she wiggled her fingers. "You're very talented," she said. "Thanks for the fun."

"My pleasure. Literally."

He strode away, well aware she was staring at his ass.

Damn fine woman.

Cleaning up in the toilet only took a couple of minutes. He had just stepped back into the room when the click of the main apartment door closing rang loud in the room. "Rose?"

The few paces it took to cross the room and open the exit door made it clear his beauty had decided to avoid any awkward after-sex chatter. Somehow she'd gotten dressed and escaped in under two minutes.

He checked the stairs and along the hallway to the next set of apartment doors, but she was gone. Nothing left but a handwritten note dropped on top of his clothes.

Safe travels home.
Rose

Chance dressed then returned to the pub for one futile walk-through, searching for her. Nothing, as he'd expected. He returned to the cabin his brother had lent him for his brief visit and fell into bed.

What seemed to be minutes later, a lush kiss woke him, heating his body and bringing a smile to his face. "Rose."

Chance rolled toward the goddess then jerked upright when he realized the sheets were cold and he was alone. No one was there except visions of his spectacular dream woman running through his mind.

Still, it wasn't as if all they had was the one night. For now, maybe. But summer was coming. The thought of it brought a whistle to his lips as he got his few things together and loaded them into his car.

He knocked once then shoved through the door of his younger brother's cabin.

"Give me tea before I go." There was no one in the main room, so Chance paused outside the bedroom and pounded the door with his fist, hard. "Wake up, Cinderella."

A muffled curse drifted back from the other side. "Go away."

Chance chuckled before he made his way across the room to the small kitchen and went to work on their drinks. He put on the kettle, found a teapot, then searched for what he needed for the coffee maker. "I thought you ranch types were all about getting up at the crack of dawn. Snap to it, brother. I want to hit the road before the traffic picks up."

Cody made it out of his bedroom a few minutes later, bleary-eyed and cranky. "I was up until three, and this was my one morning of the week to sleep in. You're a jerk."

"I'm your big brother. I'm supposed to be a gobshite. Want

me to toss a couple eggs in the pan for you while I'm making my breakfast?" Chance hit the On button on the coffee maker and turned to gather supplies from the fridge.

"Sure. If you had to wake me, you might as well cook for me." Cody moved into position by the coffeepot, staring at the liquid filling the pot as if willing it to move faster. "You're annoying on many levels this morning. Cheerful, awake, all that sort of thing."

Chance broke two eggs into the pan at the same time and grinned as they landed perfectly. "I had a good night."

Even with that opening, Cody failed to take the bait. Useless until his first cup of coffee, Chance remembered.

"Sit down before you fall down," he said with amusement.

Cody didn't argue, which said something about how exhausted he had to be. "Sorry I couldn't go out with you last night. Next time you come, give me more warning, and I'll make sure we can hit the town together."

"Next time I come, I'll be moving here," Chance reminded him, resisting the urge to ask if his brother knew Rose. There would be time enough for that later.

Cody folded his arms and frowned as if focusing hard. "You're really serious about moving to Heart Falls? Not that I don't want you around—I would enjoy the hell out of it. But this doesn't seem like the art metropolis you usually gravitate toward."

"I'm serious. Plus, I think you need to look around at how much your little town is changing," Chance pointed out. "You might still do a lot of things with a handshake and a nod, but with how close you are to Calgary, and how many people are moving out onto acreages, it's a different world. You know this. You're working on a dude ranch that caters to serving visitors."

"I guess."

No, Chance had thought this through. "Having a gallery here would make it a destination stop, but more than that, with digital sales booming, setting up in Heart Falls means I get prime real estate without the costs associated with a big city." He poured his brother a cup of coffee and placed it in front of Cody before prepping his own tea with a shot of milk. "I've enjoyed living in Europe and Ireland, but I'd like to return to Canada for good. Plus, for some unknown reason, I've missed being close to you."

"Same, bro. Your damn accent has gone back to what it was when you first moved to Canada. Makes it feel as if you've been gone even longer than it was." Cody took a deep drink of the scalding liquid before shaking his head. "I look forward to having you around. You're not gonna miss the travel?"

"Nothing says I can't travel still. But I want to settle, Cody. It's time."

Settling had nothing to do with tolerating reduced circumstances and everything to do with grabbing all the good things he'd postponed until now. The roots of a community and owning a home. The full-time companionship of his brother instead of passing moments.

Perhaps even a bold woman in his life to keep him on his toes.

He raised his cup at Cody. "I'll be here for Canada Day. I can't wait."

His brother's grin widened. "Want to jump into local life from moment one?"

"Of course."

Cody's eyes sparked with amusement. "I'll make sure of it."

Even though all the warning signs were there of something being up, Chance was too happy with his plans to ask. "Do your worst. I'm ready for anything."

4

———

July 1, Heart Falls Community Centre

Satisfaction whirled inside as Rose made the final adjustments to the table decorations for the Heart Falls Canada Day community event.

A.k.a. children's games, a family gathering, a communal potluck, and for some reason, a bachelor auction. It was the strangest combination of events, but somehow, Heart Falls made it work.

Bonus, it meant income for her. The payment for providing decorations for the tables and stage would cover most of this month's expenses. Which meant, in a few hours, she'd have another successful event under her belt and the entire month of July to sock away extra money.

A little extra to tuck away was important. Last month she'd overheard Mr. Jordon confirm he was retiring and closing his photography shop—which meant the space next door to Buns and Roses that she'd been eyeing for years would be up for grabs. It would be the perfect opportunity to expand Buns and Roses.

July was shaping up to be amazing. Wonderful and everything she'd hoped for.

Her love life was still boring, though, and seemed to be stuck that way. The one night of bliss she'd stolen kept rolling through her brain more often than was helpful. Especially since every time she remembered what she'd done, she had to keep biting her tongue to avoid spilling the beans to her sister or her friends. Other than Petra, who had gotten the limited-edition, condensed-digest version the following morning, no one knew.

Nope, that night was a lovely part of Rose's history now. She was glad she'd gotten to enjoy the experience, but now she was ready to focus on the other things in her world that needed to be taken to the next level.

After the potluck and pie sale were done, the tables were pulled to the side of the room. Chairs were rearranged and the auction began.

Malachi Fields, Rose's father and beloved emcee for the event, stepped onto the stage and smiled at the room. His dark curly hair was shot with silver at the temples now, but he was still handsome and very much the showman he'd always been.

He gripped the microphone in one sturdy hand and addressed the room. "Welcome to the annual Heart Falls bachelor auction. Funds today are earmarked for the Hope Fund and the Heart Falls Newcomers Committee. We want to be able to welcome refugees to their new homes and care for those who have lived in our community for years and need a hand. So bid often and be generous. Let's meet our bachelors, shall we?"

Rose didn't plan to bid this year. She had in the past, when she had specific goals—like a partner for a wedding she planned to attend. Otherwise, she knew all the local men, and while some were fun to dance with, none were long-term-relationship material for her. She'd find another way to donate to the community fund.

She let her mind drift to the week ahead and calculating how much they could offer Mr. Jordan to take over the lease on his shop. It took laughter and Tansy jostling her elbow for Rose to realize her sister was acting up.

Again. Typical Tansy.

Once Rose paid attention, it became clear Tansy was bidding wildly for all the bachelors. Like, for every single one. So far, she hadn't bought a date, but she'd managed to push the donation amounts far above what was usually paid at the event.

"Five hundred twenty-*five*." Tansy grinned at the woman in the front row who was bidding on the youngest Stone brother, Dustin. "You know you want him."

"Five-fifty. And I'm tapped out." The woman shook a finger in Tansy's direction. "Which you know because I told you that this morning when I grabbed my coffee at Buns and Roses. Sneaky pants."

"Hey, it's for the good of the community," Tansy said. Her pale cheeks were flushed red with energy and happiness.

"No more bids," Malachi announced quickly, darting a warning glance at Tansy. "Sold for five-fifty."

Rose nudged Tansy's shoulder and spoke quietly in her ear. "You've done that five times now. Upped the bid until they've reached their max and then bowed out. Dangerous game, sis."

"Not really. I mean, if I accidentally won, I'd pay up and stop. But since I might have overheard a few different conversations over the past week at Buns and Roses and pretty much know everyone's limits, it's mostly fun."

Rose gaped at her sister. "You're unbelievable."

"I know. But it's for the good of the community, so fair or foul, I'm working my magic." Tansy rubbed her palms together and grinned evilly.

From the podium, their father clapped his hands to regain

the room's attention. "I have a surprise for you. One final bachelor on the bidding docket is *two* more bachelors. I've just been handed this information and am thrilled to share it with you."

He gestured to the side of the stage. The men who had already been bid-on all stared toward the curtain.

Two new men stepped forward, one familiar cowboy and a man in a gorgeous suit. He turned to shake hands with one of the other men on the stage, his face hidden from view.

"You all know Cody Gabrielle, building manager at Red Boot ranch. He's thrilled to introduce his older brother to us. Recently returned from Ireland, I understand. Chance plans on settling here in Heart Falls and doing what he can to expand our artistic horizons with a gallery and art studio."

Her father continued speaking, but Rose couldn't hear through the rush of blood in her ears.

Chance. Ireland.

Oh no. No, no, *no*.

When the mystery man finally turned and faced the crowd, smiling warmly at the loud round of applause, Rose accepted three undeniable truths.

Chance was just as handsome as she remembered. Just as quiver inducing. And clearly, she sucked at secretive one-night stands, because someone in their small town would ferret out the information eventually.

She and Tansy sat far enough back from the stage that Rose didn't need to worry about meeting his gaze directly, which meant she got to look him over and try not to drool.

Chance had been easy on the eyes the night she'd picked him up, dressed in tailored pants and a button-down shirt. She'd seen him naked—also amazing. But dressed in that suit…

Dear Lord, she was about to fall over.

While she'd been mentally scrambling for balance, her father had started the next auction. Cody was up, it appeared, as he stepped forward and waved at the woman to the right of the stage who'd just offered three hundred dollars.

"Three-fifty," Tansy piped up.

Rose covered her face with a hand. "Please don't do this."

"Have to, I'm afraid." Without a speck of regret, Tansy counterbid until she finally shot to her feet and boldly announced, "Eight hundred dollars. And I'll double it if you throw in his brother as well."

Shouts and amused gasps echoed off the roof.

Malachi Fields glared at his daughter. "I thought we outlined the rules—no buying multiple bachelors. No sharing bachelors between bidders. Also, did we not specifically outlaw *you* from bidding after last year, when you somehow bought three dates *and* ended up with a chicken coop?"

Tansy pressed a finger to her lips and considered then shook her head firmly. "Nope. No law, unless you count that night at dinner last month when you extolled the virtues of considerate and thoughtful daughters and suggested I rethink attending this year's auction for the good of your blood pressure." She waved a hand regally around the room. "Don't worry, everyone, I checked with Mom. His vitals are as spry as a spring chicken. It seems that might have been a wee bit of hyperbole on his side, so voilà, here I am."

Their poor father was having kittens behind the auctioneer's podium. He actually pinched the bridge of his nose. "Someone remind me why I volunteer to do this every year?"

While the crowd laughed and offered suggestions, Rose shot a question at Tansy as quietly and frantically as she could. "Two guys? What are you doing?"

Tansy shrugged. "There's two of us. I'll date one, and you'll date the other. I thought it was in the interest of expediency, you know. To keep things rolling."

The retired teacher in the row ahead of them overheard and twisted in her seat to nod firmly at Tansy in approval. "I like how you think." She turned away before Rose could object and waved at Malachi to get his attention. "Don't you worry. You've got good kids here, Malachi. Two for two, Tansy says. She gets one, and Rose gets the other. And since I've got a ham in the oven I need to get home to, I'll toss four hundred in the pot on their behalf to make that an even two thousand dollars for the Gabrielle boys."

Money for the fund was money for the fund. Malachi glanced around the room. "Any higher bidders than that for our last two bachelors?"

"Going, going, gone," Mrs. Wilson shouted over him, shoving to her feet and grabbing her bags. "Lovely day, all. Thanks for the pie, Tansy. You girls enjoy flipping a coin to figure out who gets which bachelor."

5

Teasing laughter continued to dance on the air as the purchased bachelors made their way toward their future dates.

Rose was ready to vanish. If only she could disappear as easily as she had the night she'd met Chance.

Since that wasn't possible, she'd do the next best thing. She whirled on her sister and smacked her on the arm. "Did you even *ask* if I wanted to date one of them?"

Tansy wrinkled her nose. "Oops. Didn't think of that part."

"Of course you didn't," Rose complained. "Plus, where did you get all the money?"

It was easier to focus on that than the real issue. On how Chance was making his way across the stage with Cody at his side. The two of them on a slow but deliberate path that would be Rose's undoing.

Thank goodness for the community members who wanted to be introduced to Chance because he was new in town.

Oh, dear Lord, what had she done? Not today but one steamy night three months ago.

For once, observant Tansy seemed oblivious to Rose's

discomfort. She eased really close and whispered so low, no one could overhear this time.

"Karen Coleman gave me money to bid. Said she wanted a way to get it anonymously into the community. A day later, Kelli Stone did the same thing. They both swore me to secrecy, so this information stops here." She pulled back and met Rose's gaze. "Ah, hell. You're truly upset. I'm sorry. I didn't think it was that big a deal."

Rose shook her head, unwilling to let Tansy beat herself up for being an enthusiastic nuisance. "It's okay. It's not really you or the bidding."

"But I know you don't enjoy spending time with unknown people. Don't worry, we won't flip a coin or anything. You get Cody, and I'll take Chance, and we'll go dancing together at Rough Cut. Simple."

Which was sweet, and caring, and perfectly wrong. "You can't date Chance."

Tansy frowned, glancing over to where the guys had barely halved the distance between them. "I can't? Is there something wrong with him?"

He kissed like a god, had talented fingers, and Rose had enjoyed detailed dirty dreams about cornering him in a dark room and teasing him until he lost control.

Something wrong with the man? Absolutely not.

She opened her mouth to explain, but nothing came out.

Tansy's eyes narrowed. "What are you hiding? Because that's your hiding face."

She had a hiding face? Good grief. Rose managed a glare. "You're annoying."

"But smart, and I'm right, aren't I?" Her sister slipped an arm around Rose's waist and taunted, "Tell Tansy your every sordid secret."

"I know him."

"Really?" Surprise and happiness vanished a split second later into cunning amusement. "In a biblical sense?"

Rose smacked her sister's arm again. "Keep your voice down."

Tansy's jaw dropped as she backed up half a step. "Oh my God, I was joking, but it's true. You have carnal knowledge of Mr. Thousand-Dollar-Suit Man?"

"Yes." Rose hissed the word.

Her sister leaned forward. "If it sucked, we will ghost them—"

"It didn't suck," Rose snapped. Then she laughed, amusement finally drifting higher than her embarrassment. "It was amazing, but it was supposed to be a one-night stand. I never thought I'd see him again."

Tansy nodded, patting Rose's shoulder sympathetically. "Some women are meant for one-night stand greatness, some women simply—"

"Oh, shut up," Rose mumbled affectionately before Tansy could insult her pick-up skills or some such nonsense like usual. The banter between them was always meant in a loving way, but with the brothers closing in, she needed this clarified. "Chance is mine."

"No problem." Tansy waved at the two men. "Still, we can do the dance-till-we-drop solution if you want."

Did she want that? Meeting only in a public setting might mean avoiding a difficult conversation.

Too late. Cody was already there. He grinned at Tansy and offered Rose a quick tip of his hat.

"Ladies, I'd like you to meet my brother, Chance. He's a little on the stiff side, suit and all, but I promise he's a good guy under the lawyerish trappings. Even though I threw this auction his way at the last minute." Cody slapped a hand on Chance's back. "Okay, I lied. I sprang this on him ten seconds before we walked on the stage, and I've gotta say, the moment was sweet. Chance, meet Tansy and Rose."

Rose's brain had frozen on the word *stiff*. It was a good descriptor of the man she already knew, not because of his current attire but because of his—

Her gaze landed on his face as she feverishly prayed that, by some miracle, he'd suffered amnesia since they last met.

Chance tipped his chin briefly at Tansy, but all his attention was on Rose. He caught her fingers and lifted her hand to his lips. "Rose."

"*Shit.*"

The word slipped out. Impossible to hold back, really.

His lips twitched. "You have your calendar handy? I'd like to arrange our next date as soon as possible."

Beside them, Cody had stopped dead, his smile stuck as his gaze darted between his brother and Rose. "*Next* date?"

Tansy rolled her eyes then threw a companionable arm around Cody's shoulder and tugged him toward the pie table they needed to clean up. "Come on, my bachelor number eleven. You can help me box goodies while we plan when you're going to take me for a trail ride."

"Number *eleven*? Really? No wonder your dad's going grey."

Cody's voice trailed off in the distance, and there was no one to save Rose from the mess she had accidentally created.

A squeeze to her fingers brought her attention back to the sharply dressed man before her. "Rose. Are you okay with seeing me?"

She took a deep breath and let it out slowly, her gaze drifting over him. The perfect dark hair, the gentle smile. The suit—

Lordy, the *suit.*

It took strength of will to focus, and all she could do was go for honesty. "I didn't expect this," she admitted.

"Me either. At least not the auction part of it." He wrinkled his nose at his brother and Tansy, who were now laughing together as they packaged up the remaining pies. "I'll have to think of a suitably wonderful reward."

Rose coughed softly. "You're going to *reward* him?"

"Aye. Which will have the added benefit of messing with his mind since he expected me to be pissed."

She understood that sentiment completely. "Siblings. It's always a close call between wanting to wring their necks or hug them."

He chuckled, sliding his hands in his pockets and suddenly seeming a lot less sure of himself. "Rose, would you do me the honour of joining me for a picnic?"

He wasn't supposed to be here in Heart Falls, but he was. No matter how embarrassed she was that the man she'd spontaneously gotten naked with was now sweetly asking her out...

"Yes. I'd like that," she admitted.

Because maybe, just maybe, being bold enough to say yes to something big like a sexual romp meant she could also be brave enough to do this.

CODY DIDN'T WASTE A MOMENT. He waded in as soon as they were in the truck and headed back to the ranch. "You never told me you knew Rose."

"You weren't very talkative the last morning I saw you. I met her at the pub that night. We danced," Chance shared.

A very abbreviated version of what they'd done, but from the expression on her face, she'd been both surprised and glad to see him again, but the gladness had been a touch more reluctant.

He questioned his brother, "Has Rose ever dated anyone seriously before?"

Cody shrugged. "Not since I've been in town." He glanced

over quickly before focusing on the road. "It's a charity date. I don't know what you're used to, but this is strictly for fun and is meant to be very casual. You don't have to take it too seriously."

Didn't he? Everything inside Chance said this was important.

Now for the other details. Because this was happening. Settling into Heart Falls. Setting roots.

He'd purchased a store sight unseen. He had art and paintings already being shipped from Ireland that would arrive within the month. "She told me she owns a flower shop."

His brother nodded. "Yeah. Flowers and all sorts of knickknacks. It's the other half of the Buns and Roses café. Tansy is a wicked good cook and does all the baking. Limited menu, but everything is addictive and calorie rich. We can hit it tomorrow if you'd like."

"I won't have time tomorrow," Chance said. "I'm looking at houses with the realtor. But soon, I'd love to go."

Cody chuckled soft and low. "You're really doing this. No hesitation, full-on diving into the small-town life with a house, and a business, and all the rest of it."

"I am, but you forgot one of the most important parts of this new start." Chance laid a hand on Cody's shoulder. "Friends and family. I'll have you, brother, and for that, I'm thankful. It'll be good to finally make new memories as adults."

"The old memories aren't that bad." His brother held up his fist for a bump. "But damn right, you have me. What's more, you have a lot more guys you'll enjoy getting to know better. My boss's husband and his friends are the salt of the earth. We're supposed to get together one Friday in the next while. You're definitely invited."

"Thank you again." Chance leaned back in his seat and examined the fresh green growth in the fields around them. "Now for some details arising from our most interesting afternoon excursion. You're taking Tansy for a trail ride?"

"That's what she wants," Cody said. He frowned then shook his head as if changing direction. "You seem pleased about getting a date with Rose."

"I had already planned to ring her up once I was back in Heart Falls," Chance admitted. "I'll need you to help me plan a picnic spot."

"Can do."

"And I need you to tell me why taking Tansy for a trail ride doesn't make you smile."

Cody grumbled for a minute. "I'd hoped you'd lost that ability."

"My mind reading?"

"The habit of being a nosy bastard," Cody growled.

Chance laughed. "Answer the question."

His brother shrugged. "She's a nice woman, and like I said, she can cook like anything. But I like her as a friend, not someone I want to date."

Interesting. Also probably not the issue his brother considered it to be. "What class of eejit are ya? From the way she acted while you were cleaning up the food, I'd say she thinks the same of you. Don't assume she plans to jump you while you're on horseback."

"Friends is fine, but I don't want to lead her on, know what I mean?" Cody turned in the drive at the working dude ranch.

An assortment of trucks was parked near the cozy ranch-style home at the west side of the property. Here and there, people wandered the spaces between cabins, but Cody assured him the owners had booked off the July first weekend for family only. "Come on. I'll officially introduce you to everyone."

The rest of the day flew past, and the next, when an emergency trip to Calgary arose. Chance had to deal with customs paperwork immediately in person, or his shipment from his previous gallery would be stalled in Ireland for weeks. It meant he virtually signed the buyer's paperwork for his new studio in

Heart Falls without ever physically seeing the space. Thank goodness for technology, or he might have lost the deal.

When he finally made it back to town, Cody spent the rest of the evening grinning the way only an annoying younger brother could. "Chance, you're like a cat underfoot in a herd of horses. Settle down."

Impossible to complain that he usually was calm, cool, and collected, because since the auction, his system had gone haywire. He was nervous, excited, and far, far too eager.

The fates had continued to work in his favour, bringing Rose not just back into his life but back in a decisive way. Could anything go wrong when it all felt so right?

Chance fell asleep counting the hours until his date.

6

———

Sunday dawned bright and clear, the sky so blue that Chance was once again certain their picnic was being catered to by the heavens.

He had to hold himself back from showing up at her door too early.

Rose had given him directions to the back entrance of her shop off the alley behind Main Street. He smiled as he examined the long length of the building, each individual store with its own back entrance and a second door he now knew led up to apartments on the second level.

The door opened, and the most amazing scent wafted out as Rose joined him. Rosemary and tomato and rich, buttery cheese.

His mouth watered even more when he took her in. Jean shorts and a deep-blue top tied over a soft-cream shirt. Her runners were a blue checkerboard pattern, and she'd pulled her long dark hair into a ponytail. The crowning touch was a wide-brimmed straw hat with pale yellow roses tucked on one side.

She looked like a perfect summer day as she met his gaze with solid confidence. "Hi."

He reached for the blanket draped over her shoulder and the bag in her hand. "Hello. You look pretty."

She dipped in a curtsy then smiled harder. "You too."

Ouch. He grimaced as he gestured toward his rental car. "'Tis a cruel thing to say to a man who's hoping you're attracted to him. Unless you like pretty, that is."

Laughter drifted back as she paused beside the passenger door and waited for him to drop her things into the boot. "I think we established the first time we met that I find you attractive."

Good. She wasn't going to pretend the sex had never happened. He opened her door then stood back slightly. Just far enough to let her pass and yet close enough to truly enjoy the vision of her smooth brown legs sliding into his passenger seat.

"That bit of history does set a different sort of foundation for our date, and yet, I have a suggestion. If I may?" He crouched beside her open door so their eyes were on the same level.

Rose lifted a brow.

"I'm glad we had that night, but I need you to know I don't expect us to go there again today. Or tomorrow." When she frowned, he chuckled, grasping her fingers and lifting them to his mouth to gently kiss her knuckles. When he spoke again, his voice had gone thicker but remained lighthearted. "I plan for us get there again, not too many days in the future, but this is a fresh start. No expectations. Just two people getting to know each other."

She didn't exactly sigh in relief, but the tension in her shoulders faded the tiniest bit. Enough that he noticed.

"I'd like that," she admitted. "All of it. Getting to know you and the not-too-distant-future possibility of a repeat performance. If I'm being honest."

"Honesty always," he promised. "Now, I need you to help me follow the directions my brother gave me, because they're supposedly simple, but I have no idea where TWP47 means I need to turn."

He squeezed her hand then joined her in the car, waiting as she glanced at the directions.

Her lips curled upward. "This is where Cody suggested we picnic?"

"Is it not a good spot?"

She faced him, and her eyes sparkled with amusement. "Cody is obviously a romantic at heart. It's a wonderful place and somewhere you absolutely need to see if you're going to live in Heart Falls."

They headed out of town and north for the briefest time, the summer fields glowing with life. Cattle ranged in wide-open spaces, all of it making his heart swell with happiness. "This isn't so different from the grazing lands of Ireland."

"I've heard that. Scotland as well, from what people say." She pointed ahead slightly. "That's our turn."

They were headed toward the Rocky Mountains now, the huge peaks in the distance still capped with snow. The lower rolling hills close to them were verdant and the perfect setting for deities to play.

Chance smiled to himself. "Have you traveled much?"

"No. We moved here from Calgary when I was twelve, and I've been a Heart Falls girl ever since."

Chance slowed as the road increased in steepness, winding back and forth through narrow hairpin turns. "Would you like to travel?"

Rose had her nose all but pressed to the window. "I would, but you have to admit I'm not suffering living where I do."

They rounded another corner, and the valley spread before

them in a dizzying display. Chance slowed to a stop and stared in admiration. "Fantastic."

Green and gold and blue and brown. Every shade blended into a mosaic bursting with life. A river meandered through it all. The sunlight shone off the surface like a silver ribbon laced through the broad grasslands all the way to the eastern horizon.

He could have gawked for a lot longer, but Rose laid a hand on his arm. "Let's go before someone else comes. There's more to see ahead."

Only five minutes later, they were parked in a wider part of the road, close to the mountain edge. Chance draped the picnic blanket over the bright red cooler that had been the only thing Cody owned to hold their food.

Rose offered her hand and tilted her head toward a barely visible path in the tall grasses. "This way."

They had walked only a few paces when a strange sound tickled Chance's ears. The next moment a park bench appeared beside the trail.

"What on earth—good God."

He'd followed the line of Rose's pointing finger to discover the prime view awaiting viewers on the bench. A waterfall cascaded over the nearest ridge, crystal clear spray shooting out. A fine mist drenched the nearby hillside.

Chance plopped the picnic basket on the bench so he could take it all in. "Jaysus. That's brilliant."

"Heart Falls's namesake." Rose seemed delighted with his enthusiastic response. They still held hands, and now she curled in tighter to his side while explaining the lay of the land. She pointed to the north, starting with Red Boot ranch. Chance could recognize the layout of the ranch and even the small cabin he currently occupied. Rotating in a slow circle, Rose gave the names and a little background on each of the families and homes visible from the viewpoint. Tidbits about the people she knew so well.

It was an extraordinary gift. He didn't think she understood how much he appreciated the crash course on his new home.

"And in what you can see of town, you already know the community centre. That's where everything from community gatherings to dramatic events and musical performances happen. Although we don't get too many of those." She met his gaze, concern in her eyes. "You're opening an art gallery?"

"I am, but don't worry that I've settled in the wrong spot. Trust me, I think Heart Falls will share my love for beauty."

He realized he'd unthinkingly cupped her face. Stroking his thumb over her cheek. Staring into those expressive brown eyes.

She licked her lips. "Chance?"

"Hold on. I'm thanking the goddess of the falls for this moment."

A teeny crease formed between her brows, and then he was kissing her, sweet and soft for a moment. Then her taste rushed in—that intoxicating kiss he'd been dreaming of and replaying over and over in his head for the past months.

He barely restrained from devouring her.

Gentling the kiss, he backed up far enough to satisfy himself that the frown he'd seen forming was nowhere in sight. Just flushed cheeks and lots and lots of interest.

The next two hours went perfectly. They shared food and some wonderful conversation, accompanied by a few *accidental* kisses. Like when he touched his finger to the corner of her mouth to wipe away a bit of chocolate and suddenly found his lips on hers, tasting and taking and thrilling as she kissed him back.

She looked flustered when he pulled away but then smiled and returned to what she had been sharing. "We've moved slowly with Buns and Roses, but it's time we could expand. It'll be a little risky, but I think we're ready."

"I'll need fresh flowers on a regular basis at the gallery," Chance informed her. "I hope you'll be able to take on that contract. I definitely want to shop local."

"I'd love to," she said. "Thank you for asking. Regular purchases are a huge help. Plus, there's a lease on the store next door to ours coming up, and if we add that space to what we have now, we'll be able to branch into some new directions. Catering for Tansy, gift boxes for me."

"All worthy ideas. You enjoy working with your sister?"

"I do, and hopefully it will soon be *sisters*. The oldest of us, Ivy, is the vice principal at the local elementary school, currently on maternal leave. But our little sister, Fern, just finished graphic design school, so in a way, changing this up is also for her. She can join the business and come up with things she'd like to explore."

"Four sisters."

"We were all adopted, but yes, sisters nonetheless."

Chance nodded slowly. "Cody and I are stepbrothers, but not sharing blood doesn't make the connection any weaker. In fact, the day Cody asked to take my father's last name meant as much to me as it did to Da. It meant we truly were kin. A brother I'd always have at my back."

She flashed him a brilliant smile. "Exactly. We moved to Heart Falls right after Tansy was adopted as a preteen. It meant the tough parts of starting a new school were a little easier because we dealt with it together. She and I have been tight ever since."

Rose adjusted position to show him a picture on her phone of her family. The next thing he knew, she was in his lap—

Kissing him, being kissed. Nothing except for those sweet, drugging kisses, but Chance was over the moon.

An hour later, he was calling the date a win and cashing in

before she got tired of him. They packed up the remainder of the picnic and stood to head out.

Still, he couldn't resist. Couldn't let the day end yet. Chance stepped close enough to gently wrap his arms around her. "Want to see where I'll be setting up shop?"

She nodded immediately. "I'd love that."

Impulsive again—this woman brought out the best in him —he picked her up and swung her in a circle, laughter flying from them both. It felt good. It felt *right*.

When he let her feet touch the ground, Rose pushed back her hair and tried to un-muss herself. "It's refreshing to see a man excited and willing to show it. We've got too many cowboys around here, and their version of showing they'd won the lottery would be taking a deep breath and dipping their chin."

"I'm not a very good cowboy, then," Chance offered. "Too emotional."

"Must be the Irish in you."

"Maybe."

Hand in hand, they made their way back to the car, except for the part of the trail that was single file only. He caught her once more before they got in the car, pressing their bodies firmly together as he took her lips again.

Her lashes fluttered up.

"One final taste to remember my first glimpse of the water-fall," he teased.

She was quiet for the first moments of the drive, as if gathering her wits. He liked that idea—that him kissing her had been enough to scramble her thoughts.

Then she spoke and once again shared information about town. Places to go if he needed car repairs, places to avoid for food.

"I'm biased, I know, but it's the truth. Tansy makes the best breakfast treats and hearty lunches. Connie's Diner is where the farmers hang out for endless cups of brown liquid they pretend is coffee. It's a great place if you like their Monday special: eggs, toast, and hash browns."

"What's the special the other six days?"

Rose grinned. "Eggs, toast, and hash browns."

They were in town now. Chance drove slowly, making sure he turned at the correct corner to land on Main Street, headed in the right direction. He glanced at the numbers briefly but was more focused on the business names.

Miraculously, when he spotted it, an open parking space sat directly in front of the shop.

"This is it," he announced. He popped from the car and hurried around to Rose's side to open her door and help her out.

"This is what?" Rose glanced around in confusion. "Where is your gallery going?"

"Right here." Chance held up his hands to the photography studio in front of them. The place had seen better days, and he was sure the improvements he planned would make the entire block—

"*No.*"

The horror in her tone made his head snap around to check what had happened. "Rose? Are you okay?"

"No, I'm not." She waved an out-of-control hand to the west of his soon-to-be studio. "Notice anything?"

Chance took a fast examination of the road, the cars, the people. Nothing there that should have made her cheeks flush with anger.

Then he spotted it. The beautiful old-fashioned logo and writing on the picture window of the next shop over. The one next to the store he'd just purchased.

Buns and Roses.

Bollocks.

"Is this the place you were going to—"

"Yes," she snapped.

"Rose, I'm so sorry. I had no idea—"

She shot up a hand to stop him. One deep breath later, she spoke with utter politeness. "Thank you for the picnic and your support of the Heart Falls community fundraiser. Good luck with your remodeling."

Before he could say anything, she shot past him and vanished into the café.

7

Rose walked away before she did or said something she couldn't take back.

Thankfully, Tansy was hard at work and didn't have time to do more than flash a brief thumbs-up. Probably assumed the date had gone well.

Their little sister, Fern, was working the floor, though. Delivering a few menu items, cleaning up tables. Despite being in full work swing, her gaze narrowed as she examined Rose's face.

A moment later, she'd effortlessly blocked Rose's path with her full tray. "What's wrong?" she asked quietly.

Rose wanted to keep moving in case Chance followed, but Fern was a persistent bloodhound when she wanted information. Lying was out of the question in their family. "Something, but I need time to figure it out."

Fern blew her a little kiss then nodded decisively, stepping aside and heading for the kitchen. "Take your time, but not so much it makes you cranky."

"You're still the baby of the family," Rose reminded her,

helping open the kitchen door and lower the tray to the counter. "You don't get to call your big sisters things like *cranky*."

"If the boot fits…" Fern snagged her by the wrist before she could run away. "Give me a hug, then you can go be grumpy by yourself."

"I'm not going to be grumpy," Rose said. Then she snickered as even she had to admit she'd grumbled the words. "Brat."

"That's me," Fern admitted happily. She let go but looked as if she still had something on her mind. "Hey, Rose?"

"What, sweetie?" Rose wanted to go upstairs and punch her pillow a few million times to get her temper under control. But her family was everything to her. Just like Fern had offered a badly needed hug and would tease and taunt in the days to come if Rose didn't get over her anger, Rose sensed her little sister needed something as well.

Fern pulled a face then brushed at her curly hair. "Think I can convince Tansy to let me go on the trail ride? I know she paid for the date with Cody, but I have been wanting to go forever, and it's never worked out."

"I don't see why not," Rose said easily. "It's not really a date for them, just a fun outing. I can mention it if you want."

Her sister's eyes lit up. "That would be sick."

Rose fought a laugh. "That it would."

The moment of family time cooled Rose's temper enough that her pillow survived. Still, she ignored the text Chance sent asking her to get in contact. She wasn't ready to talk about her reaction yet.

Through a combination of luck and sneaking off to her room early, she avoided discussing her date in detail with Tansy.

Yeah, she totally wimped out and hid.

Monday was their first day off for their modified weekend,

though, so when Tansy finally crawled out of bed, Rose was waiting in their cozy living room. With muffins from the shop and a thermos of coffee, she was set up for a power chat about where they went now with their future.

Tansy woke up fast, eyes brightening as Rose briefly described her date before dropping the final revelation that the man—the sexy, interesting, made-her-insides-quiver man—had bought the shop next door out from under them.

"I'm not really mad at him," Rose admitted. "I'm just *mad*. We had all these plans for Buns and Roses to expand, and now they're off the books, and we have to start again. It's frustrating and annoying and frustrating—"

"And annoying," Tansy offered helpfully.

"You are the best sister in the world," Rose said suddenly. Tansy blinked in surprise, but Rose meant every word. "You're also a brat and simply enjoy taunting me, but I know it's because you love me. Your distractions always help me get back in balance."

"I know, sweetie." Tansy curled her fingers around Rose's arm and squeezed tight. She leaned back, her expression going thoughtful. "I know you're disappointed—"

"Frustrated. Annoyed."

Tansy snickered. "I am as well. But I have to say this—not getting the lease for next door might be for the best."

Shock struck hard. "What?"

Her sister made a face. "We've talked a lot over the years about expanding. We made those business plans, and you put tons of time and thought into them. I appreciate every bit of that, but lately I've been tangled in other directions. Like feeling how good it is to have two full days off a week after so many months of working nearly twenty-four seven."

"We have it in the plans to hire more staff," Rose reminded her.

Tansy dipped her chin slowly. "The plans are solid, sis. What's changed is the way I feel inside. Don't get me wrong, I love what we've accomplished with Buns and Roses, but I also wonder if there are lessons to learn from what our family has shown us. Our friends. That a slower pace of life doesn't mean we're lazy but that we're appreciating the life we get to live."

The idea shifted like pouring sand over rocks, creeping into crevasses and filling empty holes.

Tansy leaned forward. "Now, tell me more about what happened *earlier* in your date. Details, sis. Because until you got mad at the end, you were glowing. I've never heard you talk about a guy like this before."

"I like him," Rose admitted quietly after sharing a little more. "There's something about Chance that draws me. I don't know what it is."

Her sister leaned back in her chair and lifted her coffee. "To figuring it out."

Tansy's words about their business ideas stuck with Rose through the rest of the day and into the next. Put their plans on hold? Of course. That was the only immediate solution since the store next door wasn't available anymore. A move to a new location for more room wasn't a logical next step. Not after what Tansy had shared.

It was just past four o'clock on Wednesday when Tansy stuck her head into the huge cooler occupying most of the back of the flower shop. "I've locked the main doors for both shops, and once Fern and I finish loading the dishwashers, I'm headed upstairs for an early night."

Rose hurried back into the shop proper before the cooler heated up. "Are you reverting to a seven p.m. bedtime like when we were little?"

"As if the cakes for the wedding at Red Boot ranch tomorrow weren't enough, for some reason I agreed to also make individual cupcakes." Tansy yawned so wide, it made Rose yawn a second later, which made Tansy snicker. "I plan to start at four a.m. to get them ready in time. If I don't want to mix up my ingredients, I'm having something to eat and then crashing. How's your part going?"

The baking and flowers were a last-minute order they'd taken on to help a bride and groom whose wedding planner from hell had taken the money but not actually booked a single thing.

Rose eyed the buckets of flowers waiting for her to turn them into arrangements. "The shipment arrived late, so I'll be burning the midnight oil to get it done."

Tansy took a deep breath. "I'll grab a quick bite and a coffee, then I'll come back to help you."

"No." Rose stepped in and squeezed Tansy tight before tapping her lightly on the head in reprimand. "You're sleep-walking already. I'll do as much as I can today and get up early to finish, but I can't leave it all, or I won't have time to set up tomorrow morning. They'll need the flowers for pictures beforehand."

"Then we'll both be working hard in the morning," Tansy said. "Fern's taken control of the shops, and all the staff members are lined up to run without us, so we're good on that count." She paused then met Rose's gaze straight on. "You message Chance yet?"

Guilt struck. "I'm a little embarrassed to contact him," Rose confessed.

"I know, but you can't do the next thing until you get past this." Tansy's grin widened. "After seeing the way he was all but eating you up with his eyes when he swooped in at the auction, I'm fairly certain he's the type who will forgive anything, as long as you admit you had a moment."

"I did have a moment, didn't I?" Rose asked softly.

"When do you *not* have moments?" Tansy teased, dancing out of arm's reach. "I love you, sis. Truly, one thing I adore about you is that you're always honest. Emotional swings, happy or sad—you're real. Never apologize for that."

"But I should apologize for walking out on him, yes?"

Tansy nodded like a bobblehead. "When you get a chance. Ha—you already have a Chance if you want him."

"Go to bed. You're not funny."

"I am punny, though." Tansy shot for the door, cackling wildly as she escaped Rose's clutches. "See you tomorrow. Love ya."

"Love you too," Rose said as the door closed behind her.

Then she faced the wall of flowers before her. Time to make a dent in the mountain, and then during a break, maybe, just maybe, she'd send a text to Chance and invite him for coffee.

There was something there between them, no use in denying it. Of course, from experience, Rose knew the high excitement of the relationship would fade soon enough. It always did.

Still. While dating Chance might only last for a short time, she might as well enjoy every minute they did have together.

CHANCE STOOD in the middle of the empty photographer's studio and wondered how to turn this around.

Not the actual physical building. He had enough experience that the display units and background walls of the gallery would all get dealt with easily enough. Even though it had only been a couple of days, the art studio in the upstairs space was also thoroughly plotted out.

All the plans were there. Now he needed to put the sweat equity in.

Yet something was missing.

Someone.

He pulled his phone out again, feeling a bit like a stalker. Only the fact he managed to keep himself from sending Rose yet another message swayed him away from that dangerous territory.

At some point, she would contact him, and then he'd convince her the building purchase had all been an unintentional slight. Hopefully that would be enough to put a smile back in her eyes.

The way he was here, on one side of the wall, while she was there, just on the other, made everything a little more torturous. He dipped his roller in the pan of paint and loaded it for another run over the wall. If he wasn't getting the chance to get to know Rose better, at least he could knock off a few tasks on his to-do list.

The wall between the shops wasn't completely soundproof. The country music station on Rose's side was barely loud enough for him to pick up the pulse of the beat, low enough that the individual words were a muted hum. If he had music playing on his side, he wouldn't have even noticed hers, but pathetic as he was, even listening to her playlist was better than pretending she wasn't there.

A crash sounded, breaking glass tinkled, and Rose swore.

Chance dropped his roller and sprinted for the back door. He was in the alley and pulling open the back door of her shop before he could even think. "Rose?"

Cool air surrounded him as he pressed forward toward the swearing. Highly creative curse words, he noted with approval.

He tried again. "Rose, are you okay?"

He stepped into her work space in time to see her head spin toward him. She shot up a hand to warn him off. "Don't come any closer. There's glass all over the floor."

"I see that." Which meant glass all around where she stood in a pair of open-toed sandals. "Stay put. Where's your broom?"

She opened her mouth as if ready to protest then shook her head slightly. She pointed to the far wall. "Use that one. Unfortunately, this isn't the first time I've been a butterfingers."

Chance hurried to the wall and grabbed his weapon, careful to sweep everything to one side as he took a direct route toward her. The instant he reached her, he leaned the broom on the large island counter beside her. "You need to be somewhere safe."

Rose gasped and clutched his shoulders as he caught her by the hips and lifted her onto the countertop. "Chance, stop it. I need to—"

"You need to not slice yourself to ribbons," he informed her. "There are glass shards all over your feet. Let's get them off before something happens."

She lifted one foot and grimaced. "I hadn't noticed."

"Which is why I'll be helping you clean this up." He reached for the clasp of her sandal and realized his shirt was splattered with paint. The last thing he wanted was to add that mess to her already complicated evening. He stripped his shirt over his head then rolled it up carefully so the paint was all on the inside.

He had Rose's foot in his hands before he looked up to discover her staring at him, her mouth hanging open slightly.

She blinked and then lifted her gaze from his chest to meet his eyes. "I'm not sure how taking off your clothes helps clean up glass, but I'm having trouble demanding you put your shirt back on."

A delightful confession. He let a smile rise even as he focused on removing her sandals and gently brushing the glass slivers away. "Let me finish sweeping the floor before you get down."

She nodded then pointed toward the sinks. "If you bring me a wet cloth, I'll use that to make sure we've got all the shards."

"Of course." Inspiration struck, and he swept the area clear before inching his way toward the sinks. Other than buckets and buckets of long-stemmed flowers, the rest of the work space was pristine and tidy. Just the way he'd imagined Rose's territory would be.

When he returned with a wet cloth, instead of handing it over, he kept control, once again lifting her foot into the palm of his hand then washing carefully from her ankles, over her foot, to the tips of her brightly painted toes.

"You don't have to do that," Rose said softly.

"I want to." Chance twisted her on the countertop to wipe her other foot clean. His body was only inches away from hers, and the little quiver in her breathing as he touched her sent the blood pounding harder through his own veins.

Deliberately, he put the wet cloth on top of his shirt then twisted her again. This time toward him, her legs falling apart as he stepped between them and let his fingers drift along her thighs. "How are you now?"

She inhaled, her breath rattling for a moment. "I seem to be not just clumsy but slightly feverish."

Perfect. Chance slid his hands to her hips and tugged her toward him. Staring at her lips, knowing that all sorts of conversation should happen first, but damn if he didn't want—

Rose caught him by the cheeks and pulled him into the kiss. Hungry, heated. Just the way he wanted and exactly what he needed.

He slid his hands around her body to mesh them together. Heat to heat, need to need.

Whatever questions they had, this part they absolutely had figured out. They were combustible together, and he gave himself over to the kiss. Stroking with his tongue, nipping at her lower lip before sliding kisses along her jaw to a spot right under her ear.

She arched back and moaned. "We shouldn't do this."

"Do what?" he teased. "Kiss? Touch?"

Her hands were on his belt. "Why stop there?"

Chance caught her by the wrists. He waited until their gazes met. "I want you. But I don't want this unless you're sure."

She nodded. "I'm sure. Really, really sure."

8

Maybe something had changed deep in her soul when they had met back in April. Maybe it was still some of the lingering magic from the bachelor auction. For whatever reason, Rose Fields was having an extraordinary moment, and it was perfect.

She stroked her fingers over the warm skin of Chance's shoulders before slipping down his sides, palms caressing the firm expanse.

The music in the background switched from a cowboy singing about something romantic to a female singer warning she was going to bury the body where no one would ever find it—

"You're smiling," Chance noted. "And I don't think it's because of something I've done." He undid another button on the smock she always wore while working.

"I'll tell you some other time if we keep getting naked right now."

"A barter I'll accept." Chance hummed as he revealed her bra. Fingers stroked reverently along the edge of the lace. "You're so soft. So beautiful."

"I like how you're put together too," she admitted. She was down to her underwear before she remembered something important. "Do you have a condom?"

He stilled. Swore.

She raised a hand to cover her mouth, partly to keep from cursing and partly because his expression was truly amusing.

Chance lifted her chin in his hand. "Change of plans, unless you have supplies tucked away in some wee cupboard."

"There's no cellophane in here that you'd enjoy being wrapped in."

He kissed her. Devoured her, truthfully. Cupped her breasts and teased her nipples with his big, strong fingers. Driving pleasure over her as he stole her breath and dazzled her mind.

She wrapped her legs around his hips and pulled him forward, connecting the thin layer of her panties with the thick ridge tucked behind his boxers.

Chance groaned as his hips pulsed against her.

It was hot and dirty and something from a high school playbook as they rubbed together and teased and bit. She sank her fingers into the muscles of his back, arching and swaying to increase the pressure between them.

Excitement rose quickly, pleasure swelling up so quick and fast, Rose gasped with it. She clutched him tighter as the waves rolled.

Chance hissed sharply. He tightened the hand in her hair and pulled her head back, kissing her one final time.

They were both gasping for air a moment later, tangled in each other as she sat on the counter with him still between her legs.

"Rose?"

"Yeah?" It was a strange and yet comfortable sensation to be partly naked with him. To have just done something so intimate and now linger against each other. Rose had never felt such a physical connection, one that was so right.

He breathed out slowly, a rush of warm air caressing her cheek. "I'm sorry I messed up your plans for expansion."

She laughed softly. "That's really what's on your mind right now?"

"Going for another round with a proper condom is the top item on my mind, along with a hundred other ideas, but I wanted you to know."

"It was just a weird coincidence, and it wasn't your fault. Will you forgive me for walking out in a snit after we had such a nice afternoon together?"

"Already forgotten," he assured her. Only he was eyeing her with speculation as he helped her off the countertop. "Are you going to vanish if I go to the toilet to deal with the mess?"

She offered him a slightly guilty smile. "The door in the right corner. I promise I'll still be here."

By the time he got back, she'd used her shop sink to freshen up a little herself. Plus, she'd swept up the rest of the glass and searched in the cupboard for something she could loan him.

Chance whistled happily as he made his way across the floor to her side. "What's this?" he asked when he accepted the pile of fabric she pressed against him.

"Not that I mind what you're not wearing, but I keep it cool in here for the flowers' sake. If you're sticking around, you'll need a shirt."

He gave it a shake, frowning slightly at the dark blue fabric. "Why do you have men's shirts waiting about?"

She slipped another one on herself and pivoted as if she were a model. "I pick them up at the thrift shop. They work better than an apron, and they wash and wear well."

He shrugged it on, looking rather pleased at the fit. "You can dress me any time. Or undress me, for that matter," he added with a wink.

They were terrible. Rose caught him by the hand and pulled him toward the couple of chairs she had for when she needed to put her feet up. "I'm truly sorry I walked away from you the other day. I had a wonderful time showing you Heart Falls, and I shouldn't have—"

"I had a good time as well," Chance interrupted. "Let's focus on that part. And more." He leaned forward in his chair, stroking his thumb over her knuckles. "You intrigue me, Rose Fields. You've invaded my dreams, and I can't get enough of you physically. But it's not just that I get hard every time I think about being with you. I also smile, and in some ways, that makes me want to shake my head. I shouldn't be so fascinated, but I am."

"I feel the same," Rose confessed. "So what do we do with this strange compulsion to be with each other?"

"Give in to it," Chance said cheerfully. "Definitely get to know each other better. What we like, dislike. Get to know each other's families."

Everything was happening in a huge rush, yet Rose couldn't seem to summon the words to slow things down. "That sounds like dating. I think I'd like that."

"I'm invited to dinner," Chance said, "at your parents' house on Friday evening."

Rose blinked. "Okay?"

He laughed. "No, I'm not asking, I'm telling. Your father rang me up yesterday and told me to be there by half five and to bring wine. Red, something suitable to accompany buffalo stew. Then he laughed for some reason."

Oh, for heaven's sake. Fern must have made some assumptions, then said something at home, and now her family was staging an intervention.

Rose straightened slightly, slipping her hands from his. "You're going to my parents' for dinner? *This* Friday?"

"I am, and I desperately hope you'll be there. Because, from the glimpse I got of your father at the auction, I'd like you around as backup. And maybe Tansy, because your sister seems to have a deft hand at dealing with him."

The thought that her father could intimidate this confident man made her smile. "Is this when I should warn you that it's not the masculine side of the equation you need to worry about?"

"Your mum?"

Rose nodded and then smiled wider. "And my grandma if she's there."

"Mothers are always the most protective ones." Chance dipped his chin. "I stand warned." He glanced around the room. "It's late, but it looks as if you've got a lot on your plate."

She nodded. "It sometimes happens."

"Can you use an extra set of hands?"

The offer was unexpected but so sincerely offered that Rose paused and considered. "I caught you in the middle of something. Painting, I think."

He shrugged. "It can wait. Teach me what I need to do, and I'll help with whatever busywork is appropriate."

"Thank you. If you're serious, I'd love your help."

Chance was an eager student, and the arrangement was simple enough that with him helping gather and prep materials, the bouquets went together smoothly. They ordered a pizza so they could keep working through dinner.

The entire time they worked, they talked. Laughed. Shared.

The attraction between them was undeniable, but so was this. The easy way it felt to tell him stories. To share about growing up in a small town, about finding connections in their family that were made of choice instead of birth. She told him about her oldest sister and her brother-in-law, Ivy and Walker, and the entire family's excitement about them having recently adopted three children.

Chance shared more about moving to Canada as a teen and

how, after so many years of being a single child, Cody was added to his world.

"It took a bit, but after the first growing pains, I grew to appreciate him beyond measure. Family is everything," Chance told her. "I traveled and lived away, but we always stayed in touch. Always thought of each other because we couldn't imagine not. That's what family means to me. A gift I didn't expect to receive."

"That's not always the truth for everyone, but the Fields family is like that as well," Rose agreed. "Of all of us, Tansy had the most trouble believing we were never going to give up on her, but now she's the biggest family cheerleader."

"She was older. That made it tougher?"

"Maybe," Rose considered. "I do remember that when we figured out we had the same birthday, the same year, Mom decided that made us twins. I think that made us feel as if we had something special. *Someone* special. It was the start of us being friends. Sisterhood came later."

"That's lovely."

When they finally closed shop four hours later, ninety percent of her tasks for the wedding were done.

He paused at her side as she reached for the light switch and prepared to lock up. He turned her in his arms then tucked his fingers under her chin. "I had a good time tonight."

"Thank you for saving me," Rose said. "Both from the glass and from having to work until midnight."

"No problem." He leaned in but paused before their lips met. "A good-night kiss?"

Closing the distance between them felt natural. Felt right.

And while she'd enjoyed all their kisses up until now, this one was sweet and tender and caused disturbing flutters deep inside. When he left with a wink and a smile, Rose stood there for a moment, fingers pressed to her mouth.

Slightly bemused that fate was definitely in charge of her world.

9

———

Chance stopped on the front porch of the large family home, wine bottle at the ready. He stood a little straighter, preparing himself for—

The front door opened before he could put his hand on the oversized knocker. A young woman with wildly curly black hair popped up in front of him like a cheerful jack-in-the-box. He recognized her from Rose's family pictures as the youngest sister, Fern.

"Hi. You're here. Come in."

Fern stepped back and allowed him in far enough to close the door.

"I just got home myself," she said as she twisted to remove an oversized backpack then began unpacking it. Art books, drawing pads, a prosthetic arm with a black glove on the hand.

"Can I help with anything?" Chance offered.

She hung up the bag then turned to offer him the pile of art supplies. "Sure. Bring these with us? I'll take my arm, though. Need to charge it."

Chance accepted the pile of books even as he stole a closer look at her arm. "Very nice. Is that a myoelectric device?"

She raised a brow. "Oh, now that's intriguing. The gallery owner knows bionics."

"Not really. A number of artists I commission work from wear prostheses, but that's about all I know," Chance told her.

She motioned him forward. "This way. Charging station is in the dining room next to the kitchen. That's where Rose will be."

The competent young woman marched ahead of him, briskly passing through rooms that made him want to slow down and linger. The dining room held a massive table completely covered with gardening supplies and painted boxes. The narrow room after that held floor-to-ceiling bookcases and two cozy chairs tucked into opposite corners. Everywhere, there were pictures of family, most of them unscripted and unposed.

They marched toward the kitchen where singing drifted on the air, and the smells of rosemary and something sweet teased his senses. He stepped through the arched entrance, and a rush of images flooded him.

The kitchen. A family room. French doors wide open onto a garden blooming with colour. More chairs and tables, all in small, intimate gatherings.

Rose stood at the stove. Fern slipped past her to the corner of the next room. A slim woman with pale blonde hair worked at the taps, head cocked to one side as she held a phone in place and chatted quietly.

"Chance. So good to have you here." The somewhat familiar voice of Malachi Fields turned Chance's attention to the left. Rose's father strode forward and pressed an oversized bowl into his hands. "Shuck these, please."

"Come. There's a chair here." This time it was a much softer voice, and Chance turned to see the older woman who had to be Rose's mother gesturing toward a stool at the kitchen island. "I'm Sophie. Here's the pot for the peas." She patted him on the shoulder and then marched away, lifting her phone and instantly resuming a conversation. "How much blood are we talking about?"

The rest of the conversation was lost as she moved out of hearing range.

Chance bemusedly settled on the stool and began working on the bucketload of peas he'd been handed.

Someone nudged his shoulder. "I see they put you to work already," Fern teased.

"I love work," Chance insisted seriously.

Fern laughed then turned to her sister. "What do you need help with, Rose?"

"See what's in the garden for salad?" Rose suggested.

"No problem. See you later," Fern said to Chance. She grabbed a bowl and took off through the French doors.

Malachi was back. "Impressionist or Renaissance?"

The question came out of the blue. Chance turned from the sweet domesticity and refocused his brain. It had to be a question about what kind of art he planned to display at his gallery.

He tossed back, "Modern. Classical. Digitally enhanced in some cases. Sometimes hand illustrated, sometimes computer generated. Sometimes good old-fashioned oil, acrylic, or watercolour."

"Fascinating." Rose's father settled on the stool next to Chance. Malachi reached into the pot of peas and began helping pop the small green buds into the cooking pot. "Digital, you said. You'll have to let Fern know. Amongst other things, she's done background art for games."

"That is interesting." Ideas spun in Chance's brain, but now wasn't the time to get distracted because Malachi was already talking about books. Specifically, the store they owned and ran in town: Fallen Books.

"You're welcome to come by anytime. I'm trying to start a men's book club," Malachi said. "The ladies were easy. We offered wine and dessert, and we're filled to capacity every time."

"It's the kid-free evening that hooked them," Sophie called from the other room.

Chance let his grin loose. "Beer and books could work just as well."

"Possibly. Plus pie. Or pizza, but pie might work better." Malachi looked thoughtful. He rose to his feet and paced away, muttering to himself.

For the first time since Chance had walked into the house, silence fell. A peaceful quiet broken by gentle laughter.

"You should see your face," Rose teased.

He twisted on his chair to find her still at the stove. "I've only met four of you, but it feels like a lot more."

"We can be intense, but we're friendly. It'll get quieter once Ivy shows up. We still tend to behave better when she's around, and we're trying to be good until her adopted kids settle into the family a little more." Rose moved the pot off the burner and walked over to say hello. "I'm glad you're here."

"Me too." A hit of shock arrived when she wrapped her arms around him and pressed their lips together, but Chance got with the program fast enough. He kept his focus on the sweet gift of her greeting and ignored the thought that at least one family member had to be about to swoop in and interrupt.

"Kissing in the kitchen already? Damn, I'm impressed." Tansy entered the room and cocked a hip against the counter beside them.

Chance liked her. He liked the way Rose talked about her sister, and it was clear they totally had each other's backs.

Which meant teasing Tansy was an absolute necessity.

"I have a lot to live up to," he said. "Miss *I'll Double the Money If You Toss in the Brother*."

She snickered. "You looked as if you'd be amusing."

"Definitely. I live for danger."

Rose laughed softly, stroking her fingers over the back of his neck. "A two-for-one sale is always a good idea."

"Except the time two skunks decided to take up residence in the backyard," Tansy offered helpfully.

"I hope Cody and I rank higher than that."

Tansy pushed past them, peeking into the pots lined up on the stove. "Go show him the yard," she ordered Rose. "I'll take over here."

"Don't worry," Rose assured him. "No skunks."

He experienced another moment of shock when Rose took him by the hand and guided him outdoors to explore the garden. A few minutes later, he met the final sister, Ivy, plus her husband, Walker, and their three kids: Carter, Chloe, and Harper.

The next hours were a blur of conversation, eating, and being shown everything from the carrots the youngest child had dug out of the garden (three times) and then replanted, to Fern's sketchbooks. Rarely was Chance with more than one member of the Fields family at a time, and he was never with anyone for more than ten to fifteen minutes before someone else interrupted and stole him away.

Three hours later he sat on the adult-sized swing set, Rose swaying beside him with a happy smile on her face. His stomach was full of good food, and his head buzzed from all the bits and pieces of information the family had shared. The questions they'd asked him had been thoughtful but always open-ended. As if politely giving him the opportunity to bow out at any moment.

He gazed thoughtfully at the woman beside him. "It's been a wonderful evening."

She swung a little harder, leaning back and lifting her feet. "I like my family, but we do tend to follow our own path. Because of Ivy's social anxiety and health when she was younger, a family dinner has never meant massive gatherings around the table. Our more chaotic routine sometimes spooks people."

"I liked it," Chance admitted. "I got to have real conversations with each of them, instead of one person taking over or having to guide the topics."

"Exactly." Rose hummed a happy tune as she swung.

Chance sat on his own swing and watched her, his gaze tracing the line of her legs as she pumped back and forth.

She was so full of life, so intensely beautiful, he wasn't certain he could behave like a mature adult and give their relationship the time it needed to develop. The urge to say something wild about how much he already cared was strong.

He was drawn to her, intrigued—

Falling under her spell.

It was too fast, even though in his soul, he knew it was right. Which meant, somehow, he needed to plan and plot to make sure she felt the same way. Make sure this summer was filled with the magic needed not just to set up his studio and a new home, but a new life.

One full of opportunities to see Rose bloom.

10

———

The first gift arrived the next morning.

Rose went downstairs to grab the newspaper before hurrying back up to their apartment with the oversized envelope in her hands.

"What's that?" Tansy asked.

Carefully, Rose used a letter opener to slit the top of the legal-sized envelope. "No idea, but it's addressed to me and has no stamps. So somebody local put it through the mail slot."

She eased out two pieces of cardboard, sliding them apart to display a dazzling photograph of a bouquet of yellow roses. It wasn't a straight-on portrait but one taken at a slightly off angle. The bright yellows and pale shadows contrasted sharply, the background image a gentle blur that somehow made the flowers pop until she swore she could touch them.

"Oh. How pretty."

"Someone's sweet on you," Tansy teased. "And someone is very talented. Look." She pointed at the logo on the back of the picture.

A stylized *C* and *G* overlapped with the words *artistic*

endeavors forming waves like an old-fashioned postal script behind it.

Happiness warmed Rose. "That's Chance's logo."

"Chance and Rose, sitting in a tree, K-I-S-S-I-N-G," Tansy chanted, but she grinned widely as she wrapped an arm around Rose's shoulder. "I think he's nice, and more than that, I think *you* think he's nice."

"I do. But we're just dating," Rose said. "There's no guarantees this is going anywhere."

"True." Tansy leaned forward and examined the picture a little closer. "Those are your roses. From your shop."

Rose blinked then took a second look herself. "You're right."

He must have snapped it the night he'd rescued her from the broken glass and stayed to help.

She propped the picture on the bookshelf where she could see it easily.

That was the beginning. Every day, something arrived to make her smile. None of the trinkets were expensive, many of them free or homemade. A pretty rock he found while exploring, a bouquet made from delicate willow branches tied with rustic twine.

A small metallic button with a teeny painted frog in the middle. Around the edges were the words *I Get Up at the Croak of Dawn.*

After that first morning, Chance accompanied his offerings, and every time he showed up to present them, Rose caught herself staring at him, wondering if he would vanish soon. If the sweet wonder of their situation would fade, or if he'd realize small-town life wasn't what he was looking for.

A small part inside her worried he'd realize *she* wasn't what he was looking for.

But he kept coming.

He invited her to join him at the movies, accompanied her on walks. Occasionally they met in the evening, but more often, they took to stealing time out of the middle of the day, joining each other for lunch.

Two weeks after he'd had dinner with her parents, Chance showed up at the flower shop with lunch for them both and a book neatly wrapped with familiar wrapping paper.

Rose pushed aside the project she'd been working on so he could spread out the food. "What'd you buy at Fallen Books?"

"It's not mine. I stopped in to see your father, and he said your special order had come in. I offered to deliver it."

She paused in the middle of undoing the tape. "You were visiting my dad?"

"I was," Chance said agreeably. "You want the ham and cheese or turkey with cranberry sauce?"

Rose hesitated again. "You didn't get those at Buns and Roses. Tansy never makes turkey sandwiches during the summer."

"So I've heard. But you said they're your favourite, so I made them myself." He unfolded the paper and placed the sandwich on her plate then handed it over. He laughed when she sat without moving, laying a hand over hers and squeezing. "Rose? Are you away, love? Drifting with the fairies?"

Love. A shiver ran up her spine.

It was only an expression, though, so she pulled herself together. There were a lot of interesting things to unwrap just from this visit, and she didn't mean the package. "Did you need to order some books? Is that why you went to the shop?"

"I wanted to look around again. Your parents run a quality independent store. It's impressive." He picked up his sandwich. "Your father and I chatted. Books, art, community events. I might have volunteered to run an art night for men. Photography, painting. My areas of expertise to go with his attempt to encourage a books-and-beer outing."

"Art night for the *guys*?" Rose considered, picturing her

friends' husbands and boyfriends sitting down to such an event. "That's fresh and new for this area."

"It is." Chance grinned. "We'll have pizza and beer as well, so I assume we'll get some blokes coming out for that alone."

"Tansy just got the freestanding pizza oven she ordered. She was thinking about running a pop-up once a month in different spots around town. You might be able to sweet-talk her into cooking for the guys' night out."

He held his sandwich with one hand so he could slip the other around her waist and hold her close. "I'd prefer to sweet-talk you and have you do the convincing. If you'd consider it."

Cuddling under his arm simply added to the coziness of their intimate moment. "I could be convinced."

"Ah, the woman wants to be persuaded to work her magic. Any ideas what kind of encouragement this would take?" His words stole over her like a caress.

Another thing about him that she was already addicted to. He tangled her brain into mush with zero effort and made her senses sing with a single touch.

She lifted her sandwich slightly. "You made my favourite lunch. I'm already feeling positively motivated on your behalf."

Deals were made, plans arranged.

Between the usual hours needed to run Buns and Roses and the time she spent with family over the next week, Rose found herself juggling more and more to be able to sneak in time with friends *and* find moments to spend with Chance. Being with him seemed as natural and as necessary as breathing.

The first Monday in August, Tansy was supposed to take off for the trail ride with Cody and Fern. Only, that morning, Rose found her sister curled up on the couch with a box of tissues beside her.

Tansy lifted watery eyes to meet her gaze. "I feel terrible."

Shoot. "Summer colds are the worst," Rose said with sympathy. "Want me to call Cody and cancel?"

Tansy waved a hand. "Fern's been looking forward to it so much, canceling would break her heart. Tell her and Cody to go ahead without me."

"Okay. Can I get you anything?"

"Tea, and then I'm going back to bed." She sneezed violently four times in a row. "*Groan.* My head is going to explode."

Rose made the calls for Tansy, brewed some tea, and then, after tucking her sister into bed, headed downstairs to track down Chance.

One month. It had only been one month since he'd arrived in Heart Falls for the second time, and yet crossing the short distance between their shops had become a habit.

She knocked on the back door of the gallery. When he answered a few seconds later, he was once again covered in paint.

"You're dressed for the office," Rose teased. "Thankfully, paint splatters look good on you."

He pulled her into the shop, careful to keep his body leaning away even as he tilted his head closer. "I do seem to have a uniform, don't I?"

She brushed a kiss over his lips, soaking in the happy sensation. She checked his fingers for paint before threading hers through his and tugging him into the wide-open space of the gallery.

Half the lights were off, but the layout was now clear. Short sections stuck out at intervals from the side walls, alternating with a central core of freestanding partitions. The openings created a maze with plenty of wall space that enticed a person to keep walking, keep discovering new treasures around the next corner.

"It's intriguing. Somewhat mystical. Like wandering

through an enchanted garden maze." Rose spoke softly as she meandered forward.

The gallery was still bare-bones, with nothing displayed on the freshly painted walls. Pale green and creamy white, the look was peaceful and fresh.

The storage room at the back behind the *Private—Staff Only* sign was a different matter. Dozens and dozens of packages and tall wrapped objects were neatly organized in rows. The shelves lining three walls were more than half-full with everything from vases to sculptures to still-wrapped lumpy objects.

Curiosity bloomed, and Rose's fingers itched to peek at all of it.

"When is the official opening again?

"August twenty-seventh."

"Will you be done in time? It seems so quick."

He lifted his shoulders easily. "I have a wide variety of art on hand and three galleries in western Canada that I can contact for additional work. I'll have time, but I might steal Fern from your shop temporarily. I'll need the help not just setting up but in the studio upstairs. I think she'd be perfect."

Rose hesitated. "Oh."

"It's working with computers and art," Chance said softly. "I thought that might appeal to her, and it'll be a big help to me."

"It's probably right up her alley," Rose admitted. "It's kind of you to think of her."

"She impressed me," he said simply. Chance linked their fingers. "But if I plan to hire her, I need to hurry up and nail down the theme for the show. I want an idea that suits Heart Falls."

"Theme?"

He waved a hand at the open space around them. "For the show. I'm not featuring a single artist this time but an eclectic mix including all sorts of mediums. That means it's even more important to pick a theme that will unify the collection. I have one idea I'm working with, but it's...not quite right."

Rose nodded slowly. "I do that in the shop. Grouping collectibles in a way that makes sense."

"You do it all the time in your floral art as well," Chance said smoothly. "Every one of your bouquets suggests a different emotion or a heartfelt wish. They're brilliant."

Pride notched higher, along with a sweet joy that he'd noticed her work in such detail. "Thank you for the compliment."

He dipped his chin. "It's true."

They finished the tour then made plans to get together for supper and whatever else came up. Which might mean finishing the evening at the cabin he was using at Red Boot ranch.

Once thoroughly kissed farewell, Rose went back to work.

If she spent time daydreaming about exactly what flowers she could put into an arrangement that said, *I think I want this to last forever—*

Well, she didn't have to admit that to anyone. Maybe not even herself.

Guys' night out had finally arrived. Chance looked around at the loud, boisterous group of men gathered in the studio space above the gallery with satisfaction.

There were eight of them there that first Friday of August. His brother, Cody, and the two men from Red Boot ranch: Zach and Finn. Two from Silver Stone ranch: Luke Stone and his best friend, Tucker Stewart. Finally, a couple of men who worked as volunteer firefighters in the community: Alex and Ryan.

They'd had pizza and beer and plenty of time to talk. Now Chance was ready to make them work for their supper.

He was still figuring out the connections between them all, but from the jeering and teasing going on, the men were good-naturedly willing to give anything a go for one night.

Even something as off-the-wall for them as picking up a paintbrush.

Alex held one in the air. "You sure you don't have a drum for me to bang on instead of a piece of canvas?"

"You're good with a brush," Ryan told him. "Oh, wait, that was a *scrub* brush. My bad."

"I can paint," Zach announced. "Or so Julia tells me."

"Walls don't count," Finn deadpanned.

"They were very artistically done walls," Zach insisted.

Finn lowered his beer and stared at his friend. "They were *brown*. Not beige or mocha or cinnamon or umber. *Brown*."

Amused chuckles sounded from the group, then Luke turned to Chance. "We promised we'd try, so what are we painting? Because frankly, I drew a barn once, and it looked like a whale."

"I can draw a whale and make it look like a barn," Tucker offered before leaning toward Finn. "I'm kind of impressed you know that many other names for brown."

Finn raised a brow and a middle finger.

They both grinned.

"I think we need to start with painting by numbers. Then at least I can make it look like something." Cody shook his head. "You got all the talent, bro. I occasionally draw well enough that people can tell what it is, but it's never realistic. My stuff usually looks like comic images instead of a photograph of the scene."

"You don't really expect us to make anything worth hanging on a wall, do you?" Tucker leaned back in his chair and picked up his beer again.

"Probably not, but who knows? Embrace imperfection and jump right in." Chance explained the technique they'd be trying then glanced around at the gathering. "You can't do this wrong. Just have a go, and we'll see if there's anything worthwhile when we're done."

They all still hesitated, brushes held tentatively in the air.

He tried again. "Here's your Irish courage. Drink another beer and pretend you're on the pig's back."

Cody choked. "Where? *What*?"

Chance laughed. "It means *in a mood to celebrate*. Listen up. It's time to be decisive. Take action."

He picked up his own brush and loaded it with paint. A dozen bold strokes later, he had enough paint on the canvas to see energy come alive.

Once movement started around him, he ignored the others and continued, lured in by the swoop and slide of colour. By the excitement of letting go and following the ideas whispered in his ear by his muse.

When he finally put down his brush, conversations had once again picked up around the room. The occasional burst of laughter. A hum of approval or someone puzzling out a challenge.

Zach shook his head as he poked his brush at his canvas, but Cody slapped him on the shoulder and nodded in admiration. "That's good. I can see your cabin at the ranch. And those are the mountains beyond the arena."

Finn leaned over and examined the painting. "Well, damn. Not too shabby, Zach."

"One success story tonight, at least," Tucker said. "Mine, not so much."

Luke studied his friend's art for a moment then grinned. "You painted a castle and a dragon. I like it."

Tucker rubbed at his mouth before snickering. "Try hay bales and a kitten. I like your interpretation better. Let's go with that."

The howls of laughter echoed off the roof.

"How surprising. A rose." They'd finally settled down, and Ryan gestured to Chance's painting. "I think your subconscious is telling you something."

Deep rumbles of amusement struck as Chance whipped his head around to examine his own painting closer. Background colours of muted greens, gold and pale pink blended into a hazy summer field, but the main image, front and center, while somewhat abstract, was clearly a single deep-red rose. "Well, I'll be damned. You're right."

"Say that again. I like the sounds of it," Tucker said with a smirk.

"Painting roses. Must mean something, right, Chance?" Zach teased.

He stared at the painting, the truth smacking him upside the head. "I'm in love with her."

Absolute silence came back. Which would've been frightening, except, as Chance glanced around at their faces, every one of the guys was grinning from ear to ear.

Cody shook his head in disbelief. "You say that as if it's a surprise."

The fact parts of Chance's brain were still tumbling into comprehension was enough to keep his mouth shut. He'd known she was special. Known he wanted more.

Love? Of course it was love.

Thankfully, not one of the men around him seemed upset by how quickly he had fallen. To the contrary, the guys shoved him ahead at full force.

"Now the question remains, what do you do about it?" Tucker raised a brow. "It's time to be decisive. Take action."

The repeat of his earlier words made Chance grin. "I'll get right on that. Suggestions?"

"Buy a big bouquet of flowers, go down on one knee, and spill the beans." Cody shrugged. "Works in the movies."

"Do you suggest I buy the flowers from her and have her wondering what I'm doing, or piss her off by buying them elsewhere?" Chance asked dryly. He considered again. "You really think I should bring flowers to a woman who owns a flower shop?"

Finn shrugged. "I bring horse-related things to a woman who loves horses all the time. It seems logical."

"Kelli wants me to do things with her," Luke volunteered.

His comment was greeted by a chorus of masculine hoots.

He rolled his eyes. "Yeah, not that. Jerks. I mean, yes *that*, but also other than sex. Love languages, that sort of thing. Some people like gifts; some like acts of service. You know. Plus, Kelli likes when I let her do the things she wants to do."

Tucker's grin widened ever more. "You were doing well there for a minute then veered right back into amusing territory."

Luke threw his empty beer can at Tucker's head. "Ass."

"But he's right." Cody looked thoughtful. "If you're serious about this, figuring out what makes Rose tick is important."

"She bought me one year," Zach offered unhelpfully. "At the bachelor auction, I mean."

Just the mention of it made Chance's blood heat. "Your point? And I'd tread carefully if I were you."

The other man's cheerful visage never wavered. "She bought me so I could dance with her at a wedding." A dramatic sigh escaped him. "Then she politely manoeuvred it so there was zero chance for a good-night kiss, and she pretty much hit on my car."

Chance was lost. "Your *car*? What the feck are you talking about, mate?"

"Delilah," Zach said brightly. "I'll let you meet her later if you'd like."

"Just don't expect to get to drive her," Finn said blandly. "Mind if I interpret my best friend's not-so-solid attempt at reassuring you?"

"Someone should," Cody complained.

Despite his frustrations, despite the change of everything in his life and the uncertainty of the one thing he was really hoping for, Chance had to admit this was entertaining and satisfying. These men, this night, being so easily accepted into their midst.

Zach's words suddenly made sense as Chance's brain

worked out the puzzle. "Let me take a stab. You're saying Rose is a woman who knows her mind. She won't be pushed by rote or ritual into simply saying yes if she doesn't want to."

"Exactly." Zach leaned forward. "So why don't you just be yourself and tell her what you're hoping for?"

Be himself. It was a shockingly simple solution.

One that would take hours and hours to actually follow through on, but hopefully in the end, it would succeed in convincing Rose what she'd come to mean to him.

Chance enjoyed the rest of the evening, albeit a little distractedly. But the instant the last of his new friends left the studio, he pulled out a canvas and went to work.

12

Two weeks before Chance's gallery opening, Rose woke up on the wrong side of the bed, mad about being mad.

The entire day that followed, she forced herself to be kind to her customers. To keep a smile on her face when what she really wanted was to go hide in the shower and have a good long cry.

Nothing was seriously wrong. Only the steady shipments delivered to the rear entrance of Chance's shop had more than doubled in the past week. After spending time together nearly every day the entire six weeks of summer, it was clear he was more distracted than usual and far more tired. As if he wasn't getting enough sleep.

Which made sense. His mind had to be tangled with details for the showing. Five days ago Rose had decided to give him space to juggle preparations for his gallery opening.

It was silly how much she missed him after only a few days. Not just the sex, although until he'd vanished into his working-overtime mode, they had been burning up the sheets. And the back room of her flower shop. *And* the backseat of the new Bronco he'd purchased.

Every time they were together, they couldn't seem to keep their hands off each other. Which was another reason to give him room. Less time having sex meant more time for him to deal with his art. Dammit anyway.

She'd stopped running over to the gallery during her lunch breaks. She'd answered his texts but kept her messages short and sweet. He'd stopped dropping by with the sweet, heart-aching gifts.

He's temporarily busy. This isn't the end, her brain insisted. *Once the show is over, we'll go back to dating, and everything will be perfect again.*

Which was oddly new. Her brain being positively biased in spite of what seemed to be the end-of-relationship blues setting in.

That evening, Rose was quietly grumbling into her tea when Tansy grabbed Rose's phone off the table and shoved it into her hand. "Call the man. Text him. Go to his cabin and jump his bones. Invade his studio. You're too happy to be this cranky."

"I'm not cranky," Rose began indignantly before sighing. "Shit. You're right; I'm totally cranky. But it's not Chance's fault. He's busy, that's all."

Tansy peered over the edge of her cup. She snorted. "Too busy to see you? *Bullshit.*"

She made the last word come out like a sneeze.

Rose rolled her eyes. "Chance and I have spent so much time together this summer, and I've loved it, but I don't want him thinking that—"

"That you like to spend every spare moment together because you're completely gone over him? Yeah, I can see how that would be a conundrum."

"Shut up," Rose grumbled.

"I know you hate it when I make sense." Tansy wrinkled her nose then spoke more softly. "Go see him. He makes you happy, and God knows why, but you seem to make him happy as well. Staying out of his hair for some undefined reason is—I hate to overuse a good word, but I'll stick with *bullshit*."

"I shouldn't *need* to see him this often," Rose complained. "We just met, really. We have lots and lots of things to talk about and find out about each other."

Understanding lit Tansy's eyes. "Oh, *that's* the problem. You think there's some time limit that needs to pass before this thing between you can be real."

"He arrived July first. It's less than two months later," Rose said. She let out a long, slow breath. "I'm in love with him, Tansy."

"I know, sweetie." Her sister shifted position until she could drape an arm over Rose's shoulders. "But here's the good part— I'm pretty sure he's in love with you too."

"I thought we were just having a wild fling. It's too soon for it to be more," Rose said again but only half-heartedly, especially when Tansy snorted. "Okay, already. It's not too soon. We should totally confess our love, move in with each other, and start a family. Right now. Today, even."

Her stomach dipped for a moment as she said it, but the sense of peace that arrived a moment later, in spite of saying such an outlandish thing—

Incredible.

A noise escaped Tansy, and Rose turned to her with concern. "You okay?"

"Yes," her sister said in a small voice. "Only, paint me blue and call me a forget-me-not, I just realized people in love do wild things. Like shacking up. You'll move in with him. I won't have to listen to you snore, or hear you complain about me putting my feet up on the coffee table, or have you hog the TV control."

Tansy was on the verge of tears. Rose wasn't too far behind, except this was, again, way too fast. "I was kidding. Please don't jump the gun."

"Just let you jump the guy?" Tansy took a quick sharp inhale. "Okay, I can do that."

Rose laughed, pulling her sister in for a hug. "You're right. Chance is a grown adult. If he doesn't have time to see me tonight, he'll tell me so." She made a face. "I need a good reason for a short visit, just in case."

Her sister hauled her to her feet. "Wash your face and put on some non-pouting clothes. I'll grab you a bag of cookies from the shop you can drop off. You know. Just being neighbourly."

"Pouting clothes? You're impossible," Rose said with deep affection.

But knowing she was loved so unconditionally was why fifteen minutes later, when Rose knocked on the back door of the gallery, there was more hope than discomfort in her heart.

Tansy loved her. Her family loved her. Maybe...

"Rose." Chance's eyes lit up when he saw her, but even the glad expression couldn't erase the tired lines at their corners.

She shoved the bag forward. "I won't keep you, but I brought you cookies."

He eyed the bag then neatly caught her by the wrist and tugged her into the gallery before shutting the door behind her. The next thing she knew, he had her pressed against the solid surface, his lips hovering over hers. "I only accept sweet treats from women who stay a while."

"Or ones who take you into dusty old storage rooms," Rose teased. She slid a finger softly over his cheek. "You have time for a break?"

"With you? Always."

He kissed her before letting her go, the sweetness lingering as he clasped his fingers around hers and guided her farther into the gallery.

The place had been transformed. "Oh, you've got most of it ready."

"Want a private tour?" Chance asked.

Rose glanced at him quickly. The words were simple, but there'd been a slight shake in his voice. "I'd love one."

I think I love you.

She shook her head as he tucked her fingers in the crook of his arm and began pacing slowly through the space. Easy to say the words in her head. So, so tough to get them past her lips.

The gallery looked completely different from the last time she'd been there. The layout was the same, but the content and how it was displayed made even the smooth vertical walls come alive.

"Walk this way," Chance suggested. He twisted slightly and allowed her to take a half step forward, leaving a prime view of the art on either side and ahead of them. "You'll have to imagine the bouquets that you'll create added to the mix, but this will be the background."

An eclectic assembly of paintings, illustrations, and digitalized prints dazzled her eyes. Colours burst all around them.

Ahead of her, a large canvas featured a castle on a fairy-tale hillside with a blue sky so bright, it sparkled and a landscape of trees and waterfalls and rustic roadways. The castle itself had a dark stain surrounding the base, and she paced closer to find the artist had created three-dimensional brambles and bushes with large, sharp thorns to guard the castle.

A trio of images of young women came next. One was familiar in a faraway kind of way. Rose searched her memory until the name *Sailor Moon* popped to mind. The character stood in a garden, a wand in her hand tipped with a bright red rose.

The next image was the partial face of another woman, just

barely out of her teens, with bright pink hair and sharp cheekbones. The cartoon drawing was so lifelike Rose paused to stare in wonder.

The third woman was also drawn anime style, with dark clothing and red accents. She was in the process of swinging a shiny red-and-black scythe over her head, red petals floating in the wake of the blow.

"They're all so beautiful." Rose whispered the words as she tugged Chance around another corner, and another. More treasure to find, more explosions of colour and energy and wide expanses of mystical worlds that were so realistic, she itched to step into them.

The curiosity she'd felt since he mentioned the show was now answered. Her cheeks grew warm. Her blood raced, her mind as well. "I believe I found your theme."

Everywhere she looked, she saw roses. And Roses.

Chance pressed his fingers over hers where they lay on his arm. "Do you mind?"

The images were everywhere, in all forms and all mediums. From all times and places. Flowers bloomed on the walls of battlements and were held in the hands of Greek goddesses. They flashed to life in fairy-tale images done in ink and paint and pastels. Old stories next to new. Red Rose and her sister, Snow White—the original German version—stood next to an enormous bear. Ruby Rose from *RWBY*, a computer game a younger version of Fern had been so excited about playing, she'd hauled her big sister into her room over and over again to show off all the exciting battles.

The Beast's rose, protected under a glass dome with a single petal still clinging to the stem, while in the background, Beauty knelt over the fallen body of a hideous creature.

"I'm astonished," Rose admitted quietly. "I had no idea there were so many pictures and people with the same name as me that you could fill a gallery with them."

"You're a wonderful muse."

His words held a strange tone, and she was about to ask what was wrong when another question escaped first. "What goes there?"

Chance froze. He swallowed hard then turned with his face as somber as she'd ever seen it. "Goes where?"

Really? She flipped up a finger and pointed to the empty space. The space that, no matter which direction she'd paced the gallery, caught her attention and drew her eye. The empty place that should clearly display the starring feature. "*Chance*, it's pretty obvious something is missing."

The corners of his lips twitched, and his eyes snapped with sudden emotion. "You want to see what's missing?"

"I wouldn't have asked if I didn't," she offered softly. Maybe he was waiting for the piece to arrive. How nerve-racking that must be. "If this isn't a good time, don't worry about it."

"Oh, I mind. In fact, it's all that's been *on* my mind," he grumbled. He caught her by the hand and all but dragged her across the room toward the stairs.

"What are you doing? Slow down. I can walk."

"Not fast enough," he returned. "I want to show you what's been missing from my life."

What? From his...*life*? "I thought—"

She snapped her lips together and held back her questions. All her effort went into keeping her balance as he hurried them up the stairs to the upper level.

The long counter on the back wall was piled high with paint supplies. The sink was full of old yogurt and sour cream tubs that had been repurposed to hold paint. Splatters of colour were everywhere, the walls, the floor, the chair to one side of the enormous easel filling the main studio space.

"There." He spun her toward the painting then jabbed a long finger at it, embracing her against his body. "That's what's supposed to be at the center of the show. That's what's supposed to be at the center of my world."

She lifted her gaze to the painting. Inside her chest, something grew and grew until she was ready to burst.

There on the canvas—it was her.

13

———

C hance had been all but possessed since the guys' night out.

He'd begrudged the energy and time it took to arrange the other works for the show, to deal with the fiddly details. He did that job first, though, and did it well as usual. The few moments he'd stolen with Rose after the gallery tasks were done recharged him enough that when he left her, he returned straight to work on the painting.

Sleep and food and everything else were shoved aside as he sought to make his message clear with his skills.

A few times he'd blinked his attention off the canvas to discover Cody in the studio, shaking his head and offering plates of food.

"It's two a.m. You're going to kill yourself trying to get this done before the show," his brother warned. "You don't need to meet this deadline, you know. Just talk to the woman."

"I am," Chance told him simply. "In the language I speak the clearest."

Cody had looked as if he had something more to say, but then he shook his head and sighed. He patted Chance on the back, shoved a bag of sandwiches into his hands, then headed out.

And now, after all the sleepless nights, Chance was finally done. His heart pounded as heavily as if he'd run up twelve flights of stairs instead of one.

Because she was here. Rose, quivering in his arms, hand held to her mouth as she stared at what he'd made.

He stepped away, reluctant to let her out of reach but desperate to see her face, her eyes. Needing to see *her* and learn if the message of his heart had come through on the canvas.

As she examined each brushstroke with her gaze, he followed along. He knew what he'd placed there, a contrast of happiness and peace and home and adventure.

He'd painted Rose in a moment of sheer relaxation, her head tilted, her face lifted toward the sun. Long black hair streaming toward the earth with wisps caught by the wind as if the fairies had come out to play. The spring barely turned to summer created a mosaic with every shade of green as a background palette. In the trees, the grass, the low bushes, and the deep moss. Mist drifted like a magical cloud from the mountainside while the blue sky reflected in the glittering water of the lake at the foot of the falls.

The lake that was shaped like a perfect heart.

That blue heart, full of bright, dancing, sunlight sparks, framed Rose. She lay at the center of everything. The lake, the painting. The gallery showing, if she'd allow it. But most of all—

His heart.

Chance folded a hand around her fingers and turned her until he could stare into her eyes. "I took a picture that first date. I used it as a guide, but I didn't need to look at it very often. My memory of that moment is clear."

"I remember too." She whispered the words, throat tight

with emotion. Her gaze darted between the painting and him. "Chance. It's wonderful."

"You mean it's *brilliant*." He brought her closer. "It's what's missing from the showcase. But only if you're okay with that."

She blinked hard then frowned for a moment, "Um. Of course. You painted it. You can do what you'd like with your work."

"No, I can't," he insisted softly. "I can't put this up and offer it for others to see without knowing you're headed the same direction as me."

She still looked confused. "Where are we going?"

The guys' suggestion to be himself echoed in his ears, and a laugh escaped. He picked her up and swung her, loving the little gasp and rumble of amusement that followed.

When he set her down, he leaned over her, pressing her back in a dip. "We're going forward together, you and me. You caught my eye, and I think you've caught my soul. I know it's quick, but from the first moment, we clicked. And this—" He twirled her upright and pointed to the image, to the love he'd tried to put into each brushstroke. "This is you in my heart. Not just in a painting, but for real."

Her eyes glistened with moisture. Tears clung to her lashes. "*Chance.*"

He pushed forward, locking his hands on her hips. "Some might think I should hold my tongue. Date you for longer and make it crystal clear that we belong. I will do everything I can in that direction, but I can't deny the words. I refuse to deny the feelings. I love you, Rose. I truly do."

Her smile bloomed. Wide and bright. "Some might say it's far too fast, but I feel it too. I have since the first moment I laid eyes on you."

Heart pounding rapidly, he let his pleasure show. "I think *that* 'twas lust."

"We do have plenty of that as well, don't we?" Rose asked as she tapped his nose with her finger. "But I mean it. Everything about our time together has felt right. That first night in the bar —I'd never done anything like that before, but with you, it seemed natural. Easy. *You* feel right, as if we were meant to be."

"Aye, I'm glad I'm not the only one." He pulled her closer, lips hovering over hers. "Kiss me?"

~

SHE ANSWERED INSTANTLY. How could she not?

Gliding into the kiss meant pressing herself against him. Giving herself over to the taste of him. The feel and heat and pleasure he brought so easily. She slipped her hands to his back and dug her fingertips in. Hard muscles flexed under her fingers, his breath unsteady as he paused with his lips once again barely in contact.

"Anywhere you need to be tonight?" he asked.

She nodded. "Right here, with you."

His expression went molten. "Good. Now, stay for a moment."

He marched across the room and jerked open a drawer.

When he pulled out a handful of condoms, Rose laughed. "I'm extremely thankful right now."

"You and me both," he said as he returned to her side and scooped her off her feet. "Confession. I've taken to hiding them everywhere."

"Like a treasure hunt," she teased.

He jerked the quilt off the couch and tossed it on the floor. When she would have dropped to her knees beside him, he kept her standing. As he slowly opened the button on her slacks and undid her zipper, Rose flashed back to that first evening. To the first time he'd taken her to such heights.

They'd had sex many times since then, but this? This was *more* than sex. His expression said it all—

It was love. Love she felt as he loosened the fabric from her hips and pressed a kiss to her navel. Another to the edge of her panties.

Love made her quiver as he wrapped his arms around her torso and pressed his face to her skin. Breathing deeply and holding her tight.

Flutters in her heart. Flutters in her belly. Chance tilted his head back, and the hunger in his eyes made her brace for action.

Surprisingly, he went slow. Another kiss to her ribs, one to the tiny bow in the middle of her bra. His fingers moved against her back, and the hooks on her bra slipped free. One strap slid over a shoulder, the cups barely clinging to her breasts.

Instinct brought her hands up, but before they landed, he caught her wrists, trapping her, baring her as the material fell away. He let go for just long enough to toss her bra aside, then he was back in control.

Tugging her toward him to nuzzle under her breast. He nipped at the curve, sending tingles of desire flying across her skin like a tangled web.

"Beautiful Rose." A hum of satisfaction escaped him right before his lips wrapped around her nipple.

The tingles grew to surges as wet heat surrounded her. Pleasure rippled against her nerve endings, an ache pulsing in her core. She arched against his mouth, not so much fighting his grip on her arms as using the hold to angle herself closer.

He nipped, teeth moving rapidly in a series of tender but devastating bites. Rose's legs quivered, unsteady as blood rushed through her veins.

He dropped her wrists and captured her torso, pressing the edges of her breasts upward to his mouth. Speeding up, more urgent now. The plunder she'd expected was suddenly back on the agenda.

"*Oh.*"

Chance lifted her off her feet and dropped her in one motion, catching her and tenderly laying her on the quilt. His grin widened.

Then it vanished. He pushed her legs apart with his shoulders and placed his mouth over her sex.

Hungry yet slow. A torment that began with his tongue then added his touch as fingers teased her entrance. Rose caught his head in her hands, curling her fingers through his hair as she closed her eyes and felt.

The sensual strokes touched every sensitive part of her sex. Easing inside, pulling out. Measured, languid rocks that mimicked the press of his tongue over her clit. Her orgasm loomed closer with every moment that passed. She cupped her breasts, fingers teasing her nipples.

A noise escaped him, and she glanced down to see fire burning in his eyes. His gaze was fixed on her hands. She laughed, the sound sliding into a moan when he lifted her hips in retaliation and increased the speed of his tongue.

"Close," she warned.

"Want to be inside you, love. Want to feel you surround me." His voice rasped roughly in her ears.

She hooked her legs around him, shocked to find naked skin. "When did you lose your clothes? Talented."

"Desperate." Chance paused to put on a condom then loomed over her, staring into her eyes as the thick heat of his cock aligned with her core. He paused with the wide tip of him nestled just between her folds.

"Yes," she whispered.

His gaze locked on hers, and he rocked forward. Sliding to the root, uniting them as intimately as two people could physically be. She felt possessed, taken, connected.

Loved.

He pressed a hand to her cheek, shifting his balance to rest over her so they glided together on every thrust. Skin to skin, mouth to mouth, pleasure driving pleasure.

She was full, expanding, reaching for release even as she wanted the moment to last forever. He adjusted his hips, and the rock of his length pressed her clit, and the rising buzz of her climax grew louder.

Over and over, while the beat of her heart grew in her ears and the edge rapidly approached.

His forehead touched hers, eyes wide open as she came. Her sex tightened around him. His focus wavered then vanished as he stiffened over her, hips pulsing as if he couldn't stop. As if this last frantic drive could bring them even closer, even more pleasure.

Aftershocks rocked her, and with each one, she laughed. His thumb brushed her cheek, air moving over her skin in a heated caress. They lay tangled together on the floor, breaths still frantic, the quilt half under them and half over.

It was strange, Rose thought, to have zero concerns. No worries at all that they had made a misstep coming to this point.

He loved her.

Chance drew a finger along her arm, his hair mussed and a contented smile on his lips. "You know, I came to Heart Falls planning to settle down, but I had no idea I'd plant roots this quickly."

Another comment that made her heart skip a beat. She pushed it aside because, right now, this was all she needed. Savouring the moment without rushing ahead was important.

"Will you miss Ireland? And Germany, and Paris, and all the other places you've lived?" she asked. She rested her hand on his naked chest, gently teasing her fingertips in circles. Needing to keep in contact. Needing the touch.

"No," he answered simply. "Because while Heart Falls is now home, all the other places are only a flight away." He caught her fingers and pressed them to his lips. "I want to show you the Emerald Isle, love. Introduce you to my world of tall tales and legends. We can drop in on my folks to say hello."

"Your parents are in Limerick." She stiffened for a second, the thought of *parents* shoving this thing between them further into the realm of *holy shit, this is real.*

Considering he'd dealt with her family since nearly day one, she needed to gird her loins.

She leaned up on an elbow and smiled down. "Brings a whole new twist to *meet the parents.* But I can't lie; I'd love to see Ireland. And the rest of your family."

"Being here with Cody is important to me. But I'm glad you have all your family close. I don't want that to change. How close you are with them."

"It never will," Rose promised. Then she waggled her brows. "We'll just drag you and Cody into the fold with us. There is no escape."

"Forewarned and accepted." He kissed her again as if he craved her, and the connection between them grew and grew. "So what happens now?"

Rose considered.

Chance scooped her up and laid her over his body like a blanket. "May as well enjoy the wait while you plan our best course of action."

She shook with laughter, settling more comfortably over him. All her soft parts nicely lined up with the warm parts of him that were solid and getting harder.

"You still have a lot to do before the show, don't you?" she asked.

He made a face. "Yes."

"Including sleep," she scolded, fingers soft as she caressed his face. As much as it sucked, it was the right thing to suggest. "Let's get Gabrielle's running strong before making any bold changes in our lives."

"Go slow?" His exaggerated confusion slid into a wink. "Can we do that?"

She snickered then rested her chin on her palms, centered on his chest. "I have a lot of work the next two weeks as well. There are these massive decorative bouquets I'm creating for a very demanding client."

"The client could stop by and supervise a few times," Chance suggested. "That way he can make sure you're doing them up right."

"Oh, and *doing them up right* would mean?"

"Naked. You, not the bouquets," he clarified as seriously as possible. Delight rose in her heart. "I hear the very best floral arrangements are created in the buff."

Laughter pooled around them. "You're trouble."

"You're mine." He said it softly. Sincerely. With his entire heart.

Everything she wanted was right here. Now to get through the next weeks so they could discover what came after.

14

———

August 27, grand opening of Gabrielle's

Was there a feeling better than success?

Chance checked the crowd wandering on the main floor of the gallery and all but gloated. Music played in the background, a wild mix of theme music from epic movies and video games with assorted country and Western thrown in for good measure.

Three dozen bouquets were on display throughout the gallery. Some of the roses were deep red, some were brilliant yellow. Others, pink or nearly blue, the wild variety of colours echoed in the sizes of the bouquets. From a bare handful in a vase painted with a dancing goddess to the foyer showpiece with five dozen long-stemmed white beauties, Rose's art fit perfectly with the rest of the show.

The artwork he'd assembled was being admired by a wide selection of Heart Falls residents, young and old. Conversations and laughter and even a few arguments rang out, and Chance was delighted by it all.

He'd invited the Heart Falls Seniors Lodge residents to an advance showing the previous day. The morning before that, the brand-new kindergarten to grade two classes had poured through the doors one after the other, accompanied by teachers and parent chaperones. Chance had acted as a tour guide that day as well, sharing stories about a handful of the pieces and sending the class home with a flyer Fern Fields had created explaining the rest.

A younger child dragged her older sister past him. "Come *on*. You've got to see the bear one. The sisters made friends with him, and then the mean gnome was going to hurt them, but—"

The rest of the story faded away as the twosome were lost to sight around the corner, but Chance had heard enough to be satisfied to the tips of his boots.

Storytelling mattered, no matter how people did it. Art, or music, or books, or flowers, or games. Or good old-fashioned fairy tales.

"It's spectacular," Rose whispered as she stepped beside him and linked her arm in his. "You must be so pleased."

"My feet haven't touched the ground for the past hour." He kissed her temple. "Thanks for all you did to make today a success."

"Teamwork," she returned.

Her head pivoted again toward the painting he'd done of her.

Community members would take a look at the portrait then quickly glance around until they spotted him or Rose and offer knowing grins.

But with her cozied up against his side? It was obvious they were together. One man nodded approvingly, while his wife sighed, romance written all over her face.

"You're going to be accosted everywhere in town after this," Chance warned. "They'll all be asking what you're doing with the transplant."

"Good thing you didn't paint a scene from our actual first meeting, or they'd know in great detail *one* thing I'm doing on a regular basis with you."

Chance laughed out loud, checking her face to appreciate the flush that made her cheeks glow with happiness. "I might paint that sometime, but not for a public showing."

"I might be willing to pose," Rose teased softly.

He shook his head vehemently. "You *in* the room while I'm working on it? Naked? It would take forever to finish the portrait."

"Are you in a rush?" she asked.

Not really. Not anymore, except for the need still beating deep inside.

She hadn't said it. The *I love you* part. She'd been sweet and demonstrative and affectionate, and he knew she had to feel it—

But she hadn't said it.

The gallery was now open, and they both should have less work, at least for a while. They could go back to officially dating, with more time together than stolen moments at the end of each day before they went their separate ways totally knackered.

The brand-new keys in his pocket were a heavy reminder that days had passed. Maybe there was a new goal they could aim at together.

Walking across the floor took time, with him pausing to chat with visitors. Answering questions about sale prices and future shows. At some point, Rose gave his hand a squeeze and went to greet someone who'd called her name.

He watched her go as he listened to the question.

Although he might not have done a great job because suddenly a weight landed on his shoulder while a chuckle rang in his ear.

Chance glanced up to discover Luke Stone stood beside him, arm around a petite, slim, dark-haired woman.

"Sorry. Distracted," Chance offered.

"Is that what staring at Rose's butt is called?" The woman grinned widely.

"*Kelli*," Luke scolded.

"Calling them the way I see them," Kelli returned. She looked Chance up and down before nodding. "He passes muster. Especially after the way I saw him drooling after my girl."

Luke gave Chance a thumbs-up. "Thank your stars, because if the girls' night out crew didn't approve, you'd be in no end of shit."

"Fair play to you." Chance tipped his head at Kelli. "I hear you're in charge of the next ladies' gathering. Pick a date, and I'll arrange a night in the studio for you to do whatever artistic endeavor you choose."

"Perfect." Mischief danced in her eyes. "Charcoal sketching of nudes sounds like fun."

"Hey, now," Luke interrupted, a crease between his brows and all amusement vanishing. "Just who are you volunteering to be naked?"

Kelli gestured toward Chance. "Well, it *is* his studio—"

"Troublemaker." Luke swung her up on his shoulder, Kelli squealing with laughter. Her husband pressed a big palm to her ass and held her in place.

"Let me down, you Neanderthal. This is a fancy art gallery, not the barn," Kelli complained, trying to lift her head enough to peer at Chance.

"We're a very open-minded gallery," Chance assured her

before winking at Luke. "If you head that direction, you'll meet less traffic."

Although the crowd currently in the building seemed thoroughly amused as Luke offered a hat tip then carried a laughing Kelli out of sight.

When the unexpected floor show left the building, Chance made his way upstairs to the interactive studio Fern Fields had taken to like a duck to water.

She had an interest and some talent in watercolour painting, which might come in handy in the future. But for this show, Chance had gone high tech. When he'd gotten the delivery of computers set up and shoved the games at her to pick her favourites from, the young woman had all but squeezed the stuffing out of him before vanishing online to get started.

The upstairs had become a second maze, but around each corner on this level was a different station set up for participation and simultaneous viewing. One or two people played at each computer or game station, and what they saw on the smaller screens showed up on the wall behind them. The linked screens allowed everyone walking past to see the digital art in real time, the fantastical worlds that were now a huge part of culture and needed to be a part of the current art story.

In the center was a wide desk they'd turned into mission control. Fern had just finished setting up a family with old-school joysticks at one of the small alcoves and came to his side to give an update.

"The stations are a hit," Fern informed him. "Especially the virtual-reality program that lets you paint along with the masters. I think you're going to have Mrs. Wilson stopping by daily to try another."

Chance took a slow turn, but here, as below, everything was running smoothly. "You've done a great job," he told her.

"I'm a great employee," she returned. She leaned toward him. "I do get the gig full time, yes?"

"Yes."

"And it's not because I'm Rose's kid sister?"

"It's because you're brilliant at what you do, and I'd prefer to have you deal with the hands-on tasks that require wire or pixels," Chance told her honestly.

"Hands-on? You mean hand and prosthesis, right?" Fern winked.

He laughed. "Yes. Exactly how you're wired, it works."

Fern looked so pleased, she glowed. "I figured as much, but it's always good to hear it."

She turned away to answer a question from a guest.

Chance spotted Cody, who had just entered the upper room. "Alright, brother? This way."

Cody waved a hand and strode forward, his gaze darting everywhere as he took in the faces and excitement. "Sorry I'm late, but it looks as if it's been a success so far."

"It's gone well," Chance agreed. He checked his brother over. "You're in a suit."

The other man adjusted his tie, looking a touch uncomfortable. "Figured it was the least I could do."

"You fed me while I painted so that I wouldn't starve. That was above and beyond the line of duty as far as I'm concerned." Chance nodded in approval, though. "It looks good on you."

"Thanks. But next time, feed yourself. I don't want to have to wear this to your funeral."

"But you'd look dashing. There is that."

Cody rolled his eyes. "Take better care of yourself."

"I intend to. And of Rose." She was at the top of the stairs with Tansy at her side, the two of them slowly approaching.

His brother caught sight of them as well. "You two are well suited. Don't fuck this up."

"You can't mess up destiny," Chance said sagely.

"That's what I said." Fern popped around the edge of the desk. "Right, Cody?"

"Fern." Cody nearly tripped over his own feet stepping backward. He scrambled to stay upright as Fern eyed him.

"That's a good look on you. But so's your cowboy gear," she offered.

His brother seemed to have lost his focus along with his balance. He opened and closed his mouth a few times then coughed lightly, meeting Chance's gaze firmly. "I'm going downstairs to take another peek at the show. Great job. Catch up with you tomorrow. Fern, we'll see you 'round."

Then he was gone, pushing past Rose and Tansy, who had stopped beside the desk.

"What's his hurry?" Tansy asked.

"Running from fate. Skipping out on destiny," Fern said smoothly. "Something like that." She grinned then all but pranced across the room to help solve a problem with a station.

Rose slid her fingers into Chance's. "What did we miss?"

"I'm not sure," he admitted. But with Rose beside him, Cody's inexplicable behaviour could be ignored for tonight. "Did you need something, love?"

"You." She leaned her head against his arm briefly then straightened. "And I need to tell you that the Krugers just followed us upstairs. They have their pocketbook out and are making noises about how it's vital they buy the canvas on the upper southeast wall before someone else does."

He somehow held back a hoot of delight. "Well, I should go see if I can relieve them of their worries."

"And some cash from their wallet," Tansy suggested with a smirk. "Go. I'll take care of your sweetie until you return."

"I can take care of myself," Rose muttered.

Chance was already moving. He kissed Rose first, sweet and deep and extraordinarily restrained, if he did say so himself.

Then, while Rose was still all flustered and flushed, he

turned to Tansy and kissed her cheek. "You're on. Hold the fort, or something Western like that."

With Tansy snickering and Rose aflutter, Chance hurried away, knowing he was rock-solid with what, and who, was truly important.

Just one final thing to make all his dreams come true.

15

———

"You know," Tansy said, staring after Chance. "We didn't do so badly after all. Not getting to expand, I mean."

Rose was still buzzing from the kiss. How could she be expected to understand that out-of-the-blue comment? "We didn't?"

Her sister lifted a shoulder. "We still ended up with an entire new shop to do more with. Me, extra catering. You, extra decorating. Fern's got a job that allows her to work with her training and build her artistic talents. All without us adding rent expenses."

It was true if they looked at it like that.

Rose peered around the room, not one bit surprised when Chance landed in her line of vision. Like a magnet, she was drawn toward him. "It's been a touch magical."

Tansy curled her arms around Rose and hugged her tight, whispering by her ear, "It's been pure magic all right. I'm so happy for you, sis. A whole mysterious prince coming from far-off lands to sweep you off your feet. You deserve this."

Rose squeezed her back fiercely. "I'm not going anywhere."

"Yes, you are," Tansy corrected. "You're moving forward, and that's how it should be. I'll miss you," she said, "but not too much, since we live in each other's pockets and you'll be at Buns and Roses every day like usual, whining about how much sex you're getting."

"You're such a brat." Rose kissed her. "And I love you."

"Then the world is as it should be." Tansy winked and shoved her away. "Now git. You're giving me sweetie-poopsie-pie cooties, and I don't want them. I like my single life, thank you very much."

Rose bounced off something, only to be captured by warm, strong hands.

"Thanks for the delivery service," Chance said. "And thanks for the great job on the catering. I'll give you more notice next time."

"Family and friends get to short order," Tansy said. She glanced at Rose then back at Chance. "Looks as if you're potentially both."

Dear Lord. Rose pushed Tansy away, hoping no other embarrassing things leapt from her mouth. "Thanks for everything. I'll see you at home later."

"Sure, sis." Tansy's amusement seemed out of proportion to the joke, even for her. "Chance, I loaded those extra items you ordered into your truck."

A flurry of winks and face twitches accompanied the words.

Rose sighed with exasperation. "Are you having a reaction to something?"

"Probably, but it won't be fatal. Night, all," Tansy said, squeezing Rose one more time before she vanished between other departing guests.

"That was odd. Even for Tansy," Rose muttered.

"Don't worry about her. Come. Your parents are in the VR booth, and I think they're about to get lost in the rose maze at the Beast's castle."

Hours later, the crowds were gone. An energy remained in the air, alive with a glow that quivered through Rose's entire system. But the voices were silent, and the upstairs studio no longer buzzed with lights and music. Fern had shut everything off then high-fived Chance, hugged Rose, and headed home with a satisfied smile.

Alone at last. Chance slow danced Rose through the gallery, the sweet scent of roses lingering on the air. It was the calm after the storm, and both had been amazing.

The song ended, and he pressed a kiss to her temple. "Are you ready to go?"

"I guess." Rose glanced around, but the gallery was empty. "Walk me home?"

Okay, she lived next door, but it was the principle of the matter.

He tugged her toward the front door instead of the back. "How about a drive first?"

Rose followed willingly and climbed into his Bronco. She waited until they were on the road before hitting the questions. "What's next? How long will you keep this show up? What's the theme for the next show? What classes are you going to hold next?"

He chuckled. "You're supposed to be tired. We'll talk about all the details later, but I thought I'd change shows quarterly to start. I don't have a set theme for the next show yet, but I'm considering something more rural. Pictures of Heart Falls contrasted with scenes from classical art to prove to the hold-outs in the community that they pretty much live in a painting, so they may as well know the names of a few of the masters. And Fern is gathering suggestions for classes, so you can check that one with her."

He turned down the road that led to her parents' home. Rose wondered if she'd missed a memo about a post-gallery gathering.

Only he passed the family house then took the next two lefts, sliding to a stop in front of a house with a single porch light lit and a *For Sale/SOLD* sign on the lawn.

Chance lifted a hand in the air, keys dangling from his fingers. "I got them yesterday."

Rose curled her fingers around them. Her heart was back to racing. "Oh."

He took a deep breath. "Come home with me?"

When he paused and lifted her travel bag from the backseat, Rose laughed. "Did Tansy pack that?"

"She did. I'm not sure if it's what you'll need to stay the night or piled high with cookies."

Rose tucked her fingers into his. "Either one works for me."

They paced up the sidewalk hand in hand, the warm August air sweet with a familiar scent.

She paused and twisted until she spotted the source. "Rose bushes."

"Lots of them," Chance agreed. He stole the keys from her, unlocked the front door, and gestured her in.

Lights clicked on behind her, and then the two of them strolled together through the empty rooms. Large living room, a beautiful breakfast nook beside the kitchen with doors that would open onto the backyard. A kitchen that would make Tansy envious. Playroom and two bedrooms down. More bedrooms up.

"You could move a football team in here," Rose teased.

He was opening the master bedroom door, so the quietly spoken words floated away from her. Still, she heard.

"That's not who I want to move in..."

This room held the only furniture so far—an air mattress fully made up with deep-purple linens and a cream-coloured quilt covered with all shades of purple flowers.

"You broke away from the rose theme," she teased, pointing to the covering.

Chance pulled her against him. "I only want one Rose in my bed."

Sweet, wonderful man.

Amusement bubbled up, starting soft but quickly growing. Unable to hold herself back, and unwilling to do so, she pressed her palms to his cheeks.

She leaned in slowly, staring into his eyes until she could no longer see, could only feel, as their lips met and the connection between them flared again.

But this time, when she pulled away, she kept holding on. Not to his face or his hands but to the sensation inside that said this was right and perfect. That it truly didn't matter how they had started, or how long ago, but it was vitally important how they finished.

"I'm getting you a housewarming present," she announced.

Chance grinned. "I love it already."

A laugh burst free. "I bet you do. I'm buying you a bed. Because you don't have one, and I only have a twin, and if I'm going to move in with you, I want something comfy. The air mattress setup is pretty, but it will get old really fast."

His eyes widened. Jaw falling open, he stood there, wordless.

For approximately three seconds.

Then he was whirling her in a circle in the mostly empty room. "Thank God," he said. Over and over and over.

Rose laughed louder, clutching his shoulders and hanging on for the ride until he finally put her feet on the floor.

He caught her hands in his. "You're really ready for that? To move in? We were going to go slow."

"It's been two weeks. That's like months in dog years. Centuries to a fruit fly. A lifetime to us. Plus, we're going to be in the bed together most nights anyway," she said truthfully.

His expression grew solemn. "As much as I love the sex, and I do love the sex, that's not what I want the most. I want to keep learning more about you. Sharing more, finding dreams to chase. I want to wake up in the morning beside you, step into each day and find new things to love about you. *With* you."

Her throat tightened. "I know it's about more than sex. It is for me as well. You've shown me over and over this summer that you care, in little ways and big ways, and I'm astonished and grateful."

He danced them slowly to unheard music, swaying her against him in the nearly empty room. "I want to have a family with you. Raise children, and enjoy your parents, and spend time with your sisters and everyone else your family pulls into the whirlpool of love you've all created."

Good description. "Your family as well. Cody, and your mom and dad when they visit."

"I look forward to it." Chance held her fingers against his lips. "Rose? Are you going to say it now? I mean, you should tell the man you're moving in with that you love him. Straight up, admit the truth. I promise I'll be here to catch you, even if it's scary."

Rose stood stock-still, thoroughly confused. "What do you mean? You know how I feel. I've said it before."

Hadn't she?

He rocked them in smaller circles now, embracing her as close as two people could be with all their clothes on. "You've said you feel the way I do. You've shown the emotion, but you've never come right out with it. I need the words, love. I need them badly."

How had she—

No, this was not the time to beat herself up. Not with the man who she was one hundred percent utterly in love with standing there, such hope in his eyes.

She'd better do this right.

She flung her arms around his neck. "Chance Gabrielle?"

"Aye, Rose Fields?"

One slow, deep breath—

She met his gaze. "You're the beat of my heart. The water in the vase. The paint on the brush. The spice in the sauce. The pixels in...some computer thingy." His lips twitched, and she continued, slowing down and quietly putting all the emotion possible into the words, "You're everything that makes waking up and starting a new day worthwhile. I love you, and I can't wait to say it to you every day from now to forever."

Chance closed his eyes, smiling sweetly as he inhaled, as if soaking in her words. "That? Was perfect."

Nearly. So, so nearly perfect. Rose twirled herself away and then back into his arms. "I have one more question for you."

He raised a brow.

"Do you want to kiss me?" she asked, low and sultry.

Heat flared again, and Chance scooped her off her feet. "Let me find us somewhere private so I can answer that question thoroughly."

He brought her down on the air mattress, and they both laughed as it swayed and jiggled under their weight.

Rose caught him against her. "I love you."

His eyes brightened, so she said it again. With words, and bodies, and beating hearts.

One more night on the way to forever.

New York Times Bestselling Author Vivian Arend invites you to Heart Falls. After the story is done, their stories go on. This series of vignettes and novellas are set in the world of Heart Falls and feature previous couples and other side characters.

Heart Falls Vignette and Novella Collection
Three Weddings And A Baby
Girls' Night Out
Rose's One Night to Forever

The Stones of Heart Falls
A Rancher's Heart
A Rancher's Song
A Rancher's Bride
A Rancher's Love
A Rancher's Vow

The Colemans of Heart Falls
The Cowgirl's Forever Love
The Cowgirl's Secret Love
The Cowgirl's Chosen Love

ABOUT THE AUTHOR

New York Times and *USA Today* bestselling author Vivian Arend loves to share the products of her over-active imagination with her readers. She writes contemporary, western, and light-hearted paranormal romances. The stories are humorous yet emotional, usually with a large cast of family or friends, and a guaranteed happily-ever-after. Vivian lives in British Columbia, Canada, with her husband of many years—her inspiration for every hero and a willing companion for all sorts of adventures.

www.vivianarend.com